Nicco

A Fake Dating Bodyguard Romance

TN SEAL Security
Book 3

Chiquita Dennie

304 Publishing Company

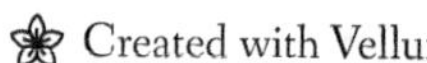 Created with Vellum

Latest Releases

Series

Struck in Love

The Early Years-A Prequel Short Story
Ruthless:Antonio and Sabrina Book 1
Savage: Antonio and Sabrina Book 2
Beast: Antonio and Sabrina Book 3
Captivated By His Love:Janice and Carlo
Brutal: Antonio and Sabrina Booke 4
Redemption: Antonio and Sabrina Book 5

Heart of Stone

Broken, Book 1 (Emery & Jackson)
A Valentine's Day Short Book 1.5 Emery & Jackson
Rebirth, Book 2 (Jordan and Damon)
Reveal, Book 3 (Angela and Brent)
Bottoms Up Book 3.5 Jessica and Joseph Short
Renew, Book 4 (Jessica and Joseph)

Cocky Billionaire Boys

Cocky Catcher (Cocky Billionaire Boys Book 1)
Bossy Billionaire (Cocky Billionaire Boys Book 2)

The Fuertes Cartel

Stolen (The Fuertes Cartel Book 1)
Saved (The Fuertes Cartel Book 2)
Betrayed (The Fuertes Cartel Book 3)

Carrington Cartel

Torn: The Carrington Cartel Book 1
Claim: The Carrington Cartel Book 2

Something

Something Gained: A Romantic Comedy Book 1
Something Earned: A Romantic Comedy Book 2

Pierce Motors

Refuel: (Pierce Motors Book 1)
Pressure: Pierce Motors Book 2)

Summer Break

Summer Nights: (Summer Break Book 1)

TN Seal Security

Aydin: Book 1
Nasir: Book 2
Nicco: Book 3

Standalones

Until Serena(HEA World Novel)
Temptation
She's All I Need
I Deserve His Love
Mutual Agreement
Scoring with Sadie
Exposed (A Bodyguard Novel)
Love Shorts:A Collection of Short Stories
Red Light District(A Fantasy Romance Short)

Disclaimer

This work of fiction contains strong language and explicit sexual content and is only intended for mature readers. This story may contain unconventional situations, language, and sexual encounters that may offend some readers. This book is for mature readers (18+).

Introduction

Grab some wine and get ready for more spicy, sinful, sexy suspense.

Are you signed up for my newsletter?

Join today and find out all the latest in new releases, contests, giveaways, sneak peeks, and more.

www.chiquitadennie.com

Synopsis

Charlie, a well-respected *Chief Designer*, and accountant at Torrio construction knows everyone has secrets, but when she uncovers secrets at work, that changes everything.

Soon, she finds herself in a terrible predicament of her own making and needs to enlist the help of a handsome former Navy Seal and his security team. But going toe-to-toe with the Mob proves much more dangerous than anyone expected.

Can Nicco and his team keep her out of harm's way or are the Mob's tentacles too long and too well-connected?

Chapter 1

Nicco

I squinted my eyes together and squeezed the trigger. Blowing out a breath, I shook my head checking to make sure the area was clear. I slowly moved in close, kicking the gun to the side. I covered Nasir while he placed the handcuffs around Jared's wrist, helping him up to stand. He limped from the wound against his leg. Our mission for today was supposed to be simple; we'd check out the location of Jared's apartment and bring him in quietly, but our luck turned into interrupting a drug deal going down with a local mobster we heard about in the area.

Nasir shut the door of the van and strolled toward the back of the apartment building, taking the gun in the bag for evidence. Police were called and informed our contact to expect Jared to be roughed up a little.

"Is he talking?" I glanced at the black van we used as Knox helped Wesley to the ambulance.

"Nah, and I doubt he's going to tell us what went down. Especially with the people he had at his place."

Nasir scanned around the back door where Jared tried to escape.

Every time we had to find someone they tried to escape and ended up getting hurt. Working at TN SEAL Security, our reputation was known as the best of the elite. Being former Navy SEALs, our skills were of high quality in catching criminals. I came to work here a little less than two years ago and being the youngest at twenty-nine, I've heard all the time how me being in position of lead on my cases so early was favoritism, but they seem to forget I put in the hours and worked my ass off to show Aydin and Nasir I could be trusted and counted on at all times. Nasir stepped into the stairwell, and I trailed along up to the apartment on the fourth floor. Living in Memphis, corruption grew from all areas in the city and some police officers we knew were corrupt. But a few still stuck to the badge and wanted to clean the city up. Pushing the door open to his apartment, I entered to see the room scattered with clothes, papers, and food boxes.

"Aydin wants us to bag any evidence and send it to the P.I.," Vaughn, another member of the team, explained.

"Toss me some gloves." I scanned the remnants of newspapers sitting on the table next to the couch. Sliding the white gloves on my hands, I picked through the papers, noticing the front page covers with the notorious Torrio Mafia family laughing together at a construction site.

Standing up, I held the paper out and motioned for Nasir to see.

"The same person in the photo." I pointed at the underboss of the family.

He jabbed a finger. "Izan Torrio," Nasir answered.

"Aydin's going to want to talk with Jared."

"They're taking him to the hospital."

"He might not make it there. I mean, let's be honest. If they left right before we busted in, no telling if they're watching us right now," I emphasized. I stalked to the window and glanced around the streets. Weather outside was cool and not too dry. People were out and about in Orange Mound, the neighborhood we found him in.

"Ambulance pulled off," Nasir mentioned.

"Have everything bagged up and sent to the office." I spoke to the team.

"Alright. I'm heading back to the office and then checking in on Cyrah."

"How is she doing with the baby?"

Nasir grinned. "Good. My boy is driving her crazy, but she loves it."

Chuckling, we left out of the apartment and back to the van, hopping in to drive to the office. "Still surprised you two are together."

"When Cyrah's mom couldn't stand me, I made it a point to try and work it out for Cyrah's sake, but I have moved on."

"She's still causing problems?"

He sucked in a breath. "Not too much. Her dad is cool."

"What do you think we'll get out of Jared?"

"You want to lead the interrogation?"

Putting the car in drive, Buckley, one of our top shooters, pulled alongside traffic. "If the police don't hold him too long," I responded.

Nasir scanned his cell phone, pushing it into his pockets. "Aydin sent a message that Jared's being discharged from the hospital."

"What about the police?"

"They're letting us have ten minutes with him."

I checked the time on my watch. "Great. Let's head to Methodist Hospital." Buckley sprang through traffic listening to the plan we wanted to operate on finding more information about the Torrio family.

* * *

We passed through the doors of the hospital room. The police nodded as they left the room, and I approached Jared handcuffed to the bed.

"Jared, we need to talk."

Blowing out a breath, he turned the tv up to drown us out. "I don't have anything to say to you."

I glanced around to make sure the door was closed. I reached over and gently tapped on his wound.

"Arggg, let me go," Jared groaned.

"You know why we're here."

He regulated his breathing. "Fuck you."

"Torrio Mafia." My features drew tight.

His eyes grew wide. "Who is that?"

I laughed at his response. "Jared, give it up."

Jared avoided eye contact. "I want my lawyer."

"Why do you need a lawyer?" I leaned forward and stared into his eyes.

A range of emotions shined on his face. "The police are right outside if you hurt me."

Taking him down as a low level for the Torrio Mafia will be easy.

"More reason for you to talk to us. We can help."

Jared's jaw slammed shut. "I'm not talking." Men like him thought they'd be protected at all times, but I had an idea he would probably go to jail for life and the Torrio family would never care.

"So, you're willing to go to jail on charges of trafficking cocaine?"

"I work a regular job in construction," Jared replied.

Slamming my hand on the railing, the machines started to beep faster. "That's bullshit and you know it!" I shouted.

Jared fussed. "Get out of my room."

"One way or another you're going to talk," I sneer at him, my teeth clenched.

The door opened, and a nurse sauntered inside holding a tray of food. "May I help you gentlemen?" She placed the food down, checking his vitals.

"I want them to leave," Jared grunted and tried to sit up to eat.

"When is he leaving?" I probed.

"Who are you?" she interrogated me, smile on her face.

I ignored her flirting. "We're here because he's a criminal."

"Well, gentleman, sorry, but Jared needs his rest." She finished putting his food together and fluffed his pillow.

"Fine, I will be back."

"I'm not talking!" Jared shouted to our backs.

Walking down the corridor, I was talking with Nasir and Buckley. We approached the elevator when we heard a loud noise and rambling of code blue. Minutes later, the same nurse came out of his room, walking in the opposite direction.

"What the fuck just happened?" I whispered. I watched more nurses and doctors head in the direction of Jared's room.

Nasir's eyes darted between me and the crowd rushing in and out. "You think it's Jared?" Nasir wondered.

"Come on." I jogged down the hall, pushing through the crowd.

"Get these men out of here!" the doctor yelled at us, and the police shoved us back.

"Is he dead?" I asked.

"Sir, are you related to the gentleman?" a nurse asked.

"What happened to the other nurse with the green eyes and dark hair?" I investigated, remembering she left through the other end of the main hall.

The doctor replied, "What nurse?"

"Nurse Leakes."

"I'm Nurse Leakes," she responded, showing me her badge. I made eye contact with Nasir. We rushed down the hall and turned to the exit doors, hearing someone rush down the stairs.

"Fuck! She must be one of Torrio's men." I sprinted down the stairs, Buckley and Nasir following behind.

"Call for backup!" Nasir commanded.

"Aydin needs to get the camera footage." Arriving on the bottom floor, I pulled my gun out and slowly opened the door, gun high up seeing security standing smoking a cigarette.

"Aye, did you two see a woman come through here in the last five minutes?" Nasir inquired.

"Yeah, she has a nice ass on her," the guard explained. I dropped my shoulders and rushed to the main entrance of the hospital, not seeing a trace of her around.

"Fuck!" I let out a breath.

Buckley's gaze scanned the building. "Come on, we need to check on Jared."

"Jared's dead and we let it happen." People rushed in and out of the hospital as the ambulance came to the front entrance with a pregnant woman going into labor.

Nasir walked back to the front parking entrance. "Torrio's behind this."

Taking my phone out of my pocket, I answered Aydin's call. "Any updates on Jared?" he questioned.

"A problem came up." I stood outside and put my gun away.

Aydin barked, "What happened?"

"He's dead." My nostrils flared.

"How?" Aydin quipped.

"I think Torrio set it up and put someone in place. How did they know he'd be brought to Methodist Hospital?" My eyes scanned the building.

Aydin said, "That's a good question. Trace back with EMTs and police on duty."

"I gotcha."

"Nicco?" Aydin asked.

"Yeah." I shifted my stance.

"It won't be the first time or the last as a lead on a case that ends up dead," Aydin informed me.

"Tell me something I don't know." We ended the call, and I stepped back in the hospital and went to the tenth floor. I approached the room as Nasir talked with the staff. Jared's body was still lying under the sheets. The doctors and nurses moved around his body.

"Any word on what caused his death?"

"Sir, we are not allowed to give out that information." The doctor examined his charts, writing on the forms.

"He had a gunshot wound and was under police custody. You need to tell me something."

"Who are you exactly?"

"This man is wanted for cocaine trafficking and other crimes."

"Are you with the police?" the doctor wondered.

"Nicco." Nasir stepped into the room.

"What do you have?" I glared at the doctor, leaving the room as the body was being removed.

"I got a still shot of her, a side profile."

"How?"

"I paid one of the guards to get it for me." Nasir held up the picture and the exact woman with long black hair and gray scrubs smiled up at the camera.

"Did you send it over to Knox?"

"Yeah, he's the best at pulling up background on people," Nasir reminded me.

"Alright, while he's doing that, I can work on talking with the EMT's and police that brought him in, because something fishy is going on for Torrio's family to know his whereabouts."

"I agree, but right now you need to calm down."

I grimaced as everyone stood around like he wasn't a high-profile patient. "Doctors might be hiding something."

Nasir chuckled and I shoved it off. "True, but right now we can't prove anything."

At twenty-nine, I took my job seriously, and after my father joined the Navy, I wanted to protect my country. After I finished my duties, I joined Nasir and Aydin at the company he built, and found that even though I didn't have to worry about going out on large missions around the world, I was still fulfilled in my work. Single with no kids or wife made it even easier, but according to my mom, it was time to settle down and get married with kids.

To me that felt like a burden to put on someone when I had a dangerous job and probably couldn't tell them some of the things we ended up doing to make it out alive.

"Yo, we're heading back to the office," Buckley announced, leading the way out of the hospital.

Staring back at the photo, I imagined she was paid a hefty amount to kill a man in broad daylight with the police right outside. Having an assassin on payroll meant nothing to the Torrio family, and the years we've put in to find something to bring them down was slowly fading away.

Once we made it back to the office, I slugged through the door, piling my coat on the back of the chair, as Molly stood at the door.

"Here's your lunch." Molly handed the bag of food over. I pushed it forward in front of me.

"Thanks, how's business today?"

"Slow. Aydin and Amelia had a meeting earlier with some big time real estate broker," Molly explained, sitting against the wall.

"More business."

"Yep, which means more time away from my baby," Molly pouted.

Molly being married with kids, and Amelia, along with Cyrah, were the women of the office. All three were like sisters to me and they tried their best to run my love life.

"How are the kids?"

She pursed her lips. "Great, but I miss them all the time."

"Aren't they in daycare?"

"Yeah, what's the point?" Molly strolled over to me

folded arms over her chest. I exhaled a breath shook my head. "Nothing."

"Maybe your grumpiness will get better once you find a wife," Molly hinted.

I gave her a look. "No ma'am."

"Anyway, Aydin said you needed me to research something?"

"Find out what you can on the police and ambulance that took in Jared today."

I handed the file over from today's assignment. "How far back are we talking?" Molly checked.

"About five years or more."

"Okay, I will get right on that." Molly walked out of my office, and I logged into my computer and scanned the photo of a nurse from Jared's room to do a background check. I removed my gun, sat back, and searched through the bag of food for a fork to start eating the lasagna, baked chicken, and salad Amelia made for the staff. Zooming in on the computer screen from the newspaper heading, I saw Torrio grinning wide at accomplishing yet another deal, pretending like he was an upstanding businessman. I settled in the chair and ran a search on the staff of their construction company as I ate, looking for a lead. Nothing stuck out. I tossed the trash away as my door opened.

"Anything?" Aydin approached me.

"Not yet."

"Keep searching. Secrets always get spilled."

Slouching in the chair, I ran a hand down my face. "I'm going to be here all night."

"Don't we have a meeting in the morning to run over the logistics of today?"

Frustrated, I blew out a breath. "Joys of a debrief meeting."

"A part of the job when you signed up." Aydin reached to pick up the file on the desk.

I checked through my email replies. Working a late shift is the last thing I wanted, especially when my brother wanted to hang out. I knew the case would take over my life.

"Maybe look into the family or kids," Aydin proposed.

"Good idea."

"Especially any offshore accounts. They could have millions and billions of dollars in their names."

"On it."

"Great, see you tomorrow."

"See you." I parted ways and he clapped me on the back and chucked my chin.

Chapter 2

Charlie

After viewing my computer, I marked up the areas I needed to double-check on upcoming accounts. For a woman, let alone a black woman, working in this business is rewarding yet challenging. I groaned at my phone ringing this early in the morning.

"Morning, Adam," I answered, sorting through emails.

"Charlie, we need you to send over the contracts for the Froster building." I drop my pen, clicking through Froster emails with a roll of the eyes.

I scanned the files. "That's not scheduled for another five months, Adam."

"I know, but Hector needs to look it over again." Adam responded.

"Hmmm."

"Listen, I have a meeting in about five minutes. Email what you have." Before I could respond, he hung up.

"He irritates me, cutting me off like that." After finishing reading the latest update from the owner and our team, I dropped the phone. My time at Torrio Construction was full of perks but filled with long hours and non-stop meetings. Despite being a billionaire developer, Mr. Izan Torrio hired me right away when I told him how my ideas would save money and increase profits in the real estate market. Coming from a smaller firm into a larger area has shown me what I'm capable of doing. It didn't hurt that his son had a crush on me. To this day he tries to ask me out, but I turned him down at every request. In five years, I rose to the position of Chief Designer and Accountant in a male-dominated business.

"Two million, that seems weird." I scanned the email correspondence again and the same thing came up.

"Charlie!"

My head whipped around at the loud outburst. "Huh?"

"I've been calling your name for five minutes. Did Adam call you?" Videl stood at the door of my office.

"Sorry, he did." I cleared my throat.

"You got the paperwork?" He checked his watch.

"Videl, are you handling the Froster account?"

"Yeah, why?" He stalked over to my desk.

Closing out my email account, I picked up the file on my desk and handed it to him. I slipped my hand in my purse for my cell phone.

I cocked my head to the side. "No reason. I just needed to make sure I added your email."

"Are you going to lunch with us?" Videl asked.

"Who's all going?" I popped a piece of gum in my mouth.

"Same group, including Cynthia, but before you say no..."

Already annoyed just hearing her name, I said, "No."

"You need to try and get along," Videl fussed.

"Have fun without me." I swung my head around to open my desk drawer and grabbed a new pen.

"It would be good for you to come to lunch."

"Why? I have lunch with you all the time."

Scanning the empty hallway, he closed the door behind him. Videl walked up to my desk and bent down.

"I heard some bigwigs are going to be there."

Videl tried so many times to get me to be social. I hung out with a few people, but Cynthia is the last person to be friends with at my job. "Like who?"

"Mr. Torrio and maybe a few other people."

"I've met Mr. Torrio before. You go and have fun."

Videl sloped his head to the left. "Charlie, being in a high position as Chief Designer means you talk to the other big people."

"I agree, but sitting at a table with Cynthia is out of the question." I smiled and went back to work on my designs.

Rolling his eyes, Videl huffed and flipped open the file on Froster. "I will have the final copy sent over later today before I head home."

"Okay, thank you."

"Truly are missing out," Videl insisted as he stood in the doorway.

"I'll pass."

I continued to finish my sketches. I was deep into my work when my stomach growled. I rubbed it, ready to eat. I put my things away and grabbed my purse and jacket. Heading out of the office, I closed my door.

"You look lovely today," Hector Torrio greeted me. I flipped my hair away from my eyes.

I cleared my throat. "Thanks."

"Where are you off to?" Hector asked.

"Lunch." I paused before I moved forward.

"My treat."

"No, thank you."

Hector slipped his hands in his pockets. "Charlie, we've worked together long enough. You still can't trust me?"

Hector's sexy smile would have any woman swooning, especially Cynthia, his assistant. Word around the office is she is his girlfriend, but I mind the business that pays me and stay out of folks' relationships.

"It would not look good for me if I'm seen out with you. Besides, you have a girlfriend."

"Girlfriend?"

"Yeah. Cynthia." I turned to walk down the hall, toward the front entrance of the building, and out to my car. Hector trailed beside me.

"Cynthia is my assistant only, no more. Now, can I take you to lunch as friends?" He paused in front of me.

I glared at him. "Co-workers only."

Elaine, the office receptionist, Cynthia, his assistant, and a few other ladies have gossiped about Hector in bed. I wasn't buying his lies.

"Co-workers, friends." Hector licked his lips.

"Hector."

He crossed his heart and raised his hands in surrender. "I promise only co-workers. Besides, I need to talk to you about some business."

I exhaled a breath and nodded. "Alright and you will be paying."

Hector held the door of the limo open. I climbed to the far right of the window and crossed my legs.

The door closed and the driver sprinted into traffic as

Hector began to speak. "How are you liking it at the company?" False pleasantries to get on my good side weren't working and I wished he'd stop.

"Great," I answered, giving him a one-word answer.

His eyes took in the expression from my face down to my toes, and I felt like he was undressing me with his eyes. "My father's impressed with you."

"Is he?"

Hector stretched his arm on the back of the seat and faced me. "You shocked?"

I hunched my shoulders. "A little."

"I'm not. He's always liked you and wants to see you go even higher."

"Why do I feel like you're buttering me up?"

"We value our employees that work hard and are loyal."

"Where are you taking me to lunch?"

"Here." Hector motioned as the car stopped at the Firebirds Wood. Working and living in Collierville, a few miles from my old stomping ground in Memphis, I've learned to appreciate living on my own after college and enjoying my lifestyle without inhibitions. My parents, Taleia and Kenny Amor, instilled in me to work hard and nothing is a limit.

Hector stuck his hand out for me to take. I hopped out and shut the door. I tried to remove my hand from his grip, but he tightened it, opening the restaurant front entrance.

"You scared people might think we're in a relationship?" Hector teased and I sighed.

"Yes, and you know what you're doing, Hector."

"Why would that be so bad?"

He glanced around the room and raised his finger in

the direction of a group of people I recognized, Videl and Cynthia with some other folks.

"Is this a setup?"

Hector tugged on my hand, checking his pocket as his phone rang.

"Be a good girl." Hector placed a hand on my lower back, but I walked ahead to put distance between us and smiled, arriving at the table. Videl started to pull a chair out for me, but Hector stopped him.

"She's good right here," Hector said and took the chair next to me.

"What are you doing here?" Videl whispered in my ear.

I shrugged. "He caught me leaving for lunch."

Videl nodded and Cynthia gave me a glare.

"I will have the numbers for Froster tonight," Hector explained.

"Isn't that the account you're working on?" I poked Videl in the arm.

"Yeah, I probably need like another hour and I can be finished," Videl answered.

Firebirds is a staple in the city for the best steaks, seafood, and pasta.

"Charlie, we haven't crossed paths outside of work in a while. Are you still dating that guy?" Cynthia asked and snapped her fingers, trying to recall.

"Single."

"Really, such a shame," Cynthia jested.

Some of the men at the table looked around, shocked at her catty remark.

"Not for me," I replied. Hector finished his call, then put his phone on the table.

"Videl, I need the final report asap when you get back to the office," Hector emphasized.

"On the Froster building?" Videl sat back in his chair.

Hector nodded."Yes, as soon as possible."

The waitress appeared with more glasses of water and appetizers for the table. "Yes, sir," Videl responded.

"I was looking at the account and the numbers seemed off."

Hector shot a look at Cynthia and back to me that I couldn't recognize. "I'm sure Videl will double check."

"True, but with my name being attached I would feel better to run it by Izan as well."

"He's too busy to handle something so little. I will do it."

"Okay."

* * *

Hours later, after listening to the same boring talks, I came home to eat and watch a movie. Finally taking my robe off, I climbed into bed. I yawned, spreading my books and computer over the comforter and lowering the TV to concentrate on securing my next big project for the Torrio family. Resting on the headboard, I logged into my work emails and work account checking all latest correspondence. Videl hadn't responded to any updates so I figured he triple checked and everything with Froster was lining up correctly. I clicked through the next file on the screen, matching the displays on my screen with my printed documents. I saw higher amounts that weren't signed off by me.

"This is weird."

Removing my glasses, I wiped my eyes and closed out of the file. I headed to account departments, and noticed the last email trails, scrolling over the numbers, and saw higher amounts with my name signed off.

"What is going on?"

Videl managing the account seemed normal, but seeing a weird number that the transfer was going in and out of seemed suspect. Saving the document, I emailed it to myself to print out and research in the morning. I pushed the computer to the edge of the bed. Tossing and turning, I couldn't sleep and crawled out of bed and picked up the computer and headed to my office. Turning the light on, I sat down and pulled up what I saved and printed out everything. I grabbed a sharpie and lined up what I originally proposed and designed against the new numbers. Picking up the phone, I dialed Videl's number, hearing it ring until he finally answered.

"Hello," Videl answers.

I clamped my teeth tight. "Videl, we need to talk."

"Charlie."

There was a wrinkle of annoyance in his voice. "I need to talk to you, in person."

"Charlie, it's two in the morning."

"I know, but something's wrong."

"Can't this wait until tomorrow?"

I buried my face in my hands. "No."

"Alright, where are we meeting?"

"Your place in twenty minutes."

"Okay," Videl agreed, then hung up.

Right as he hung up, I heard another click. I pulled the phone from my ear and stared at the phone.

"Was someone listening on the call?" I muttered.

Jumping up, I grabbed all the paperwork. I rushed upstairs to change clothes and get my purse and keys. Darting back downstairs, I opened the door, stalked to the car, and dropped my things in the seat and reversed out of the parking space. Stopping at the light, I noticed a car parked on the street in the rearview mirror.

"You're paranoid, girl." I shook my head.

Since there was not much traffic, I made it to Videl's place in under twenty minutes. I parked, turned off my car, and got out. I marched to the front door, knocking loudly when it suddenly popped open.

"Videl," I whispered.

Looking behind me, I stepped into his place. Everything seemed in order. As I walked to the kitchen with the lights off, I felt a chill down my spine.

"Videl."

No answer.

Taking a deep breath, I headed to the back of his house and lightly knocked on the door waiting for him to speak. With a squeak of the door, I moved forward. I gasped in shock to see Videl in bed with a bullet in the middle of his forehead.

"Videl!" I ran to the side of the bed, looking for the phone to call nine-one-one.

I scanned around the room and saw clothes tossed around and furniture turned over.

"911, what's your emergency?" The operator spoke.

The line went dead.

"Hello!"

The phone slipped out of my hand and I stumbled back and looked out of the window, noticing a car drive off.

Reaching into my pocket, I removed my cell to call

the police and ran into the living room and locked the front door.

Hours later the police interrogated me, and Videl's body was removed from the house as tears ran down my cheek.

"What is your relationship to Mr. Videl?"

"We work together. I already told you five times."

"Ma'am, we have to triple check all angles," the officer explained.

"How much longer is this going to take?"

"No forced entry," another officer with short gray hair said as he approached.

"Does that mean he knew the person?"

Both officers glanced at me. "We will be in touch if we have any further questions." He handed me a business card.

"Thanks." I walked over to my car. I got in and dropped my head on the steering wheel. Driving back home, I thought over the past few hours and yesterday about work.

"I need some help."

Arriving back home, I climbed out and strolled inside, turning the light on. I dropped everything in my hands at the sight of my place being destroyed.

I reached in my pocket when I felt my phone vibrate. I opened the text message.

Unknown: *Stop looking.*

Me: *Who is this?*

I dialed the number and it said unavailable.

Running back to the bedroom, I grabbed a bag and threw some clothes together to leave and stay with my friend until I could figure out what happened.

Boom!

I jumped and scrambled to the bathroom, locking myself inside with shaky hands. I hid in the shower and dialed for the police as the doorknob twisted and turned.

"Oh my god, please don't let me die," I murmured.

Chapter 3

Nicco

I kicked the bathroom door open, hearing a woman scream. Aydin followed behind me with his gun. I shoved the shower door back.

"Please don't kill me!" she begged.

I grimaced at her curled up in a ball, frightened. "Where is he?"

"I don't know what you're talking about?" Her face was ashen.

I narrowed my eyes, taking in the beauty behind the tears rolling down her face. Knowing the mission we had, I couldn't let a pretty face distract me. A flash of disgust hit me at Hector being her boyfriend.

"Where is your boyfriend, Hector?" I investigated, more pissed than I should be.

Her eyes ballooned wide. "I'm not involved with Hector," she answered.

I felt she was telling the truth, but I had to force an answer, with her being in the photos of them together and her number showing up on his phone records. "Not from what we've heard."

"Who are you? I have the police on the phone." A lump seemed to rise in her throat as she spoke the words.

I watched her climb out of the shower and smelled a waft of her perfume. "Good, maybe they can tell you how much trouble you will be in when we find Hector."

She glared at me. "Did you destroy my place?"

"Charlie, we work for TN SEAL Security, a team that handles profile cases," Aydin explained.

Charlie took a seat on the bed. "Okay, what does Hector have to do with me?"

"We have reason to believe Torrio Construction is a part of the mafia," Aydin said.

"It's true," Charlie whispered.

"What do you know?" I wanted to find Hector and his father before they left the country.

"Videl." Charlie raised her hand to her mouth, sobbing. Aydin and I made eye contact.

"Who is Videl?" I approached and handed her a tissue to wipe her face.

"He's my co-worker at Torrio. Tonight, he was killed." Charlie sniffed, blowing her nose.

"How do you know?"

"I found something strange in the accounts, so I called him to meet up tonight," Charlie explained.

"What happened?"

"Nothing. He's dead," Charlie replied.

"Shit, they might be on to her now," Aydin suggested.

"On to me how?" Charlie questioned.

I sighed. "Whatever you found in those papers spooked Hector." My pulse quickened at someone hurting her. Her dark brown skin would be a sight to wake up next to every morning. Every emotion she felt could be spoken for across her face.

"Hector wouldn't hurt me."

"Do you have someone you can stay with tonight?" Depending on her answer, I wanted to help her no matter what.

Charlie stood up. "Uhm, my friend. I can go and stay with her."

"Where are the documents?" I pressed.

Charlie bent down, lifting it up off the ground. "In my purse."

Holding it out for us both to read, she explained, "I handle the design and accounts at Torrio Construction." Charlie swiped a hand across the back of her neck.

"What made you suspicious?"

"The numbers didn't add up from what I originally proposed and now my signature is forged." She pointed at the papers.

"How many people know about your concerns?"

"You and I spoke with Videl."

"For now, you can't stay here. Obviously, they killed Videl and are probably waiting for the right moment to take you out."

"So, what am I supposed to do?" Charlie walked out behind us to her car.

"Pretend everything is the same," I emphasized.

"And you think Hector will believe me?"

"As long as you give him no reason. Videl dying means he knows you know but won't make a move unless you try something else."

"Tonight when I called Videl, I heard another click like someone was listening on our call," Charlie said.

"Pull records and I can take the first round of watching her place," I suggested.

"Let me make some calls. Still pretty early in the morning," Aydin replied.

"The more reason to catch them off guard." I stalked off to the van, watching her speak with Aydin. She started her car and pulled off to head to her friend's place.

"You believe her?" Nasir wondered.

"As of now I do."

"Remember as the lead on the case, you have to look at all angles," Nasir told me.

"You think I'm not able to run my own case?"

"I think having a beautiful woman involved can cloud judgements," Nasir responded, and I scoffed.

"Nobody involved."

He chuckled and I sat back in the van watching her home, running a background search on her and her closest family and friends.

* * *

Next morning, I yawned while drinking on a fresh cup of coffee. All night in my dreams Charlie appeared and I had to try and think of counting sheep to get my hard on to go down. Staying overnight, sitting in Charlie's home, nobody came creeping around, so I left around five a.m. for the next shift to take over. I got about five good hours of sleep and came into the office at ten a.m. ready to debrief. Molly passed around coffee from the local cafe around the corner.

"Where do we stand?" Aydin asked.

Pulling up all the files on Charlie, Hector, and Torrio Construction, I cleared my throat and spoke.

"So far everything leads to Torrio's eldest son. Based

on the information Charlie gave us, Videl is dead, basically expendable."

"The question is why?" Nasir muttered.

"He knew too much or too little," I answered with a shrug.

"Charlie is the only one that has evidence on Hector," Aydin brought up.

"Hector might want her taken out next."

"That's if he knows that she's on to him."

"So, we wait to see if he comes after her?" My brows dipped in concern.

Charlie's life meant nothing to the Torrio Mafia unless she kept her mouth shut. I had to figure out a plan to keep her safe before the entire mob figured out she's working with us.

There was a knock on the door and Molly popped her head inside.

"Aydin, someone named Charlie is here to see you," Molly said.

Perplexed, I stood right along with Aydin, walking out of the conference room to the front desk.

Charlie stood with another woman beside her, whispering together.

"Aydin, Nicco, this is my friend, Dedra." Charlie waved to the red head with a short bob next to her.

Seeing Charlie up close during the day, her beauty glowed even more as her brown skin and round oval shaped face, bold, bright brown eyes, high cheekbones, and kissable lips caused me to pause.

"Nice to meet you," I replied, extending a hand.

"Have you gone into the office today?" Aydin asked.

"No, I came here first," Charlie responded.

"I researched all of the accounts you handled for the

past five hours, still more to do, but did you know most of the accounts have your signature?"

"Are you sure?" Charlie wrinkled her nose.

"Tell us what happens after you create the proposal."

"Nicco is handling the lead on your case. We can go to his office," Aydin directed. I motioned to the first door on the right. Aydin shut the door behind us. I sat at my desk as they took the seats in front of me.

Charlie pulled out her cell phone and folder.

"I couldn't sleep last night after seeing Videl killed and what you said." Charlie laid a few papers out.

"How close are you to Hector?"

"Not close, beyond him constantly flirting to get my attention."

"He creeps me out," Dedra confessed.

"You never had a relationship with him?" I knew bringing up these questions might cause her to retreat, but I needed to know how deeply she's involved personally and professionally.

"For years, Hector has tried to get me to see him as more than the son of the boss and I shot him down every time." Charlie rubbed the goosebumps on her arm.

"After speaking with our connections at the police station, I think Videl's death was a mob hit."

She gasped and clutched a hand to her chest. "It's all my fault." I automatically wanted to hold her in my arms, but knowing Nasir might gloat caused me to throw off those thoughts.

"Why would you say that, Charlie?" Dedra asked, rubbing Charlie on the back.

"If I never called him last night, he'd still be alive."

I brushed a hand across her closed fists. "No way to know that for sure."

Charlie stood up and paced back and forth.

"Charlie, relax. We can go to the police, right?" Dedra mentioned.

"Like us, he probably has connections. Without hard evidence pointing to Videl's death, the entire thing will be a waste," I announced, shuffling through the desk.

"Are you saying I have to wait until he kills me?" Charlie barked.

Aydin hesitated on what he was thinking next, and I already knew the suggestions of how to trap Hector.

"You are a threat to the Torrio Mafia, and that means you're a liability."

"Should she leave the state?" Dedra wondered.

"From hearing what Charlie says about Hector, it sounds like he's obsessed."

"Oh my god." Charlie plopped down in the chair.

"I have a gun, and she can stay with me while you investigate, right?" Dedra countered.

"Normally I'd agree, but Hector easily got Videl killed. Hate for someone else close to Charlie come up dead," I answered.

"He's right, Dedra," Charlie agreed.

"Our team is onto Hector, but we need more time," Aydin expressed.

"My life is on the line," Charlie muttered, biting her bottom lip.

"Which is why I suggest you stay with me for the time being," I hinted, watching her eyes blink in surprise.

Silence filled the room. Aydin had no clue of my idea and I wanted to go into detail at the meeting, but plans changed.

"Stay with you." Charlie stared at me.

"I understand Dedra is your friend, but to protect

both of you, I think it would be better if you had around the clock protection."

"What do you think?" Charlie quipped, watching Aydin.

Aydin closed a hand in his pockets and agreed. "He's right. You go back to the office and play pretend so we can get him on tape and stay with Nicco."

"The team will be outside of the building and at my place."

"Are you sure this will work?"

"Also tell Hector you have a boyfriend," I added. Aydin stood motionless, baffled by my comment.

"What!" Charlie and Dedra screeched in surprise.

"Nicco, can I speak to you in the hallway?" Aydin announced. I rose from the chair, followed him out, and shut the door behind me.

"Boyfriend?" Aydin held a frown.

"I know it sounds crazy." My first thought was to go take care of Hector myself. To see Charlie that scared sent a sharp pain to my chest. All I wanted to do was protect her.

"First, you tell her about lying with you before we even discussed it and now you want to pretend to be her boyfriend," Aydin grumbled.

"It came out before I could even think it through."

"You like her."

I sighed and bit my bottom lip. "I can't explain it. Something about her makes me want to protect her."

"All it takes is one mistake to get feelings caught in a situation and you both end up dead," Aydin argued.

"I hear you."

"Do you? Because after giving you the lead on a case,

I never expected you to put yourself in direct harm's way," Aydin fussed.

"She needs us."

Aydin seethed. "Our duty is to protect, not fall in love with the client."

My lips turned into thin line, and my head cocked to the side at his comment. "Amelia." Hypocrisy rolled out of my mouth.

"That's different." He pointed at me.

I chuckled. "Charlie's not a distraction for me."

"As of right now, but anything can change."

"We need to get back inside. Charlie needs to get him on tape or at least get evidence of mafia ties."

"How will that happen if she's attached to you?"

"Easy. Men like Hector think a woman will fall for his charm, no matter if she's with someone or not. The thrill of her betrayal excites him."

"Fine, but the minute things go wrong, I'm pulling you out."

"I agree." I extended my hand for him to shake, then pushed the door open, and walked back inside to take a seat.

"Nicco and I talked. Ultimately, it's up to you if you agree about the fake boyfriend. We feel Hector would try even harder to get you if he knew about Nicco," Aydin emphasized.

"So, a fake boyfriend or I die by a mobster are my only options," Charlie jested, her widened smile and plump lips covered in red lipstick sent a spark to my dick.

"Being a former SEAL, we take our jobs seriously, nothing will happen to you," I promised, giving her my full attention.

Charlie and Dedra made eye contact, seconds later

Charlie nodded in agreement, and we started to make plans of how to take down the Torrio family.

* * *

Unlocking the door to my apartment, I ushered Charlie inside, carrying a bag of groceries and her suitcase.

She huffed, shaking her head. "I could have carried my own bags, Nicco."

Locking the door behind me, I stalked to the kitchen and unloaded the groceries on the counter. "Not while I'm around. Take a seat. We should talk and eat dinner."

Charlie stood in front of the island. "Are you sure this is the right thing to do?"

I took out the vegetables, fish, bagels, potatoes, and salad mix.

"You have no reason to really trust us. I know finding your friend killed was a lot, on top of us busting into your place."

A sadness washed over her face. "Can I help with anything?" She changed the subject.

"We should probably get you situated in the guest room. I can get dinner started and we can talk about the next steps," I proposed. She turned to grab her things and I gestured down the hall to the right guest bedroom. I pried the door open. It had a basic bed, tv mounted on the wall, and a chair with a desk in the corner. Often my little brother would stay for a visit and hang out playing the games.

"Thanks."

"Come out when you're ready." I whipped around, went back to the kitchen, and prepared some scallops, roasted peppers, and spaghetti. Growing up with both parents, my mother made sure we learned how to cook and never relied on anyone for our basic house duties. Even on holidays I helped out my mother around the house by cooking to ease some of her stress and my dad and brother took turns cooking to give her a break.

"Smells good." Charlie came into view, hair tucked behind her ear, in my gray robe and house shoes.

"I hope you don't mind. I saw them lying in the room."

I cleared my throat. "It's fine. My little brother likes to steal my shit when he stays over."

She smiled. "How old is he?"

I set the plate in front of her and reached for another to fill mine.

"Emmanuel's twenty-two."

Charlie took the drink and plate. "How old are you?" Heading to the dining room, she took a seat across from me.

"Twenty-nine and you?"

Taking the fork, she moved around the food on her plate. "Twenty-seven." Charlie moaned, closing her eyes at the food, and I shifted in my seat. Trying to take the focus off the curiosity of her taste, I directed the conversation on what steps we had to take to get Hector and his father in jail for good. For the rest of the night, we talked and went over plans of us being a fake couple for a few months to help benefit us both.

Chapter 4

Charlie

After having dinner with Nicco and establishing the details of him being my boyfriend, I called Dedra early in the morning to talk me out of the plans because no one would believe that me and Nicco had a relationship out of thin air. Nicco drove me to work. I took in his strong hands on the steering wheel and his deep brows blended together as he talked to his team on the speaker phone. The man was sexy from his long muscular arms, large hands, and sharp jawline, down to his thick, long legs. The height difference of his six-two staring down at my five-eight gave me goosebumps. When they broke into my place, not only was I upset but turned-on staring into his green eyes.

"We're pulling up now," Nicco announced.

"I have a car outside the building," Nasir answered. I looked out of the rearview mirror and saw a gray jeep a few blocks down. Nicco put the car in park and I reached for the handle, but Nicco captured my arm.

"What's wrong?"

"I'm going inside with you," Nicco responded.

"Are you sure? What if Hector's there?"

"Then it makes it even better." Nicco shoved the driver's door open, going to the passenger door, helping me out.

"Wouldn't it be weird if I bring you up here now?"

"No, pretend like your boyfriend wants to see where you work." Nicco smiled.

"You are cute when you lie."

He grabbed my hand and we moved to the front entrance of the office. Arriving early was my normal routine, so I didn't expect it to be crowded, but the amount of people standing around crying made me stop in my tracks.

"Charlie, oh my god, did you hear?" Elaine, the receptionist, took a hold of my hand.

"Hear what?" I pretended to go along with the story Nicco worked up of me not knowing Videl was dead, so the trail wouldn't have me at his place.

"Videl was killed last night. So heartbreaking. I know you two were close," Elaine said.

I gasped and laid my head into Nicco's chest. He rubbed my back. Something about the comfort of his arms around me wanted it to be real.

"I'm sorry. We haven't met. Elaine, I work as the receptionist."

"Sorry to hear about your friend. Nicco, Charlie's boyfriend," Nicco emphasized and kissed the top of my head.

Elaine grinned, and she stared a little too long at Nicco for my liking. I probably shouldn't care since our plan might be working, but I felt a certain way. Her long blonde strands, fake boobs, and heavy makeup had every guy in the office falling to have a date with her and the gossip was that Hector already had a few one-night stands but dumped her after a few months.

"Elaine, will you excuse us? I have to check in with the team upstairs." I cupped Nicco's hand tight and switched to the elevator, pushing the button for my office.

"She seems nice," Nicco rambled.

I glared at him. "She's not, it's only because you're here."

He smirked. "You're jealous."

The ding interrupted our stare off. We climbed on and I pressed the button for the highest floor and watched the numbers get bigger. I ignored his stare.

"Fake relationship already has me in the doghouse after one day," Nicco groaned, making me laugh.

"Shut up."

He reached for my hand right as the doors opened and Hector stood with his assistant and lawyer.

"Charlie, good to see you." Hector looked from me to Nicco and down to our hands.

Fidgeting next to Nicco, normally I could handle Hector's gaze, but knowing the real truth about him made me hesitant. "Uhm, hi Hector."

"I never expected you to show up today," Hector commented, stepping back to allow us off the elevator.

"Why is that?"

He shrugged. "I know how close you and Videl have been over the years."

"Yes, of course. Still can't fathom him being murdered."

"Crazy to think he was murdered, damn." Hector repeated.

"Babe, you wanted to show me your office," Nicco

interrupted, knowing I might have fucked up about Videl in the moment.

"Who's your friend?" Hector cocked his right brow up.

"My boyfriend. Honey, this is Hector, my boss's son."

"Boyfriend? Since when?" Hector held a dark glare.

"For about a year now."

Hector clenched his fist. "You never mentioned a boyfriend."

"Is there a problem?" Nicco reached for my hand and pulled his arm around my waist.

Hector dropped the smirk and pushed his hands in his pocket. "No problem here. Charlie's one of the best designers we have," Hector expressed.

"Never doubted her." Nicco pressed a kiss to my cheek, lugging me away from Hector, and I pointed down the hall to my office.

Waving at my secretary, I shut the door behind us. I slouched down in my chair and threw my hands over my face.

"He knows."

"Stop worrying."

"Nicco, he knows. I am terrible at lying."

Nicco reached out to cup my chin, lifting my face to his. "He's sizing me up and wondering how he's going to get rid of me."

"Get rid of you for what?"

"He wants you bad."

"Hector can want a billion women, I won't be on the list."

Nicco laughed and I joined in. I logged into my computer. "What are you thinking about doing?"

"For now, act normal. If you get a chance to hear

anything, take this pen and it will record all conversations."

"I feel like a spy or something."

He shook his head while I took it out of his hands and shoved it into my pocket. "Are you sticking around?"

"I have to head back to the office, but I will pick you up later."

"How long will we have to pretend?"

"Until we catch him in the act or someone spills the truth. Listen, more than Videl's murder is at stake."

Leeriness in his eyes told a story. "Me going down for money laundering."

"Yes. Unfortunately, your hands are all over the documents. Hector or whomever is trying to frame you."

Sweat coiled in my palms. "I messed up badly."

"No, you need to stop freaking out. Letting him get to you is the last thing I want for you."

"Torrio Construction is having an annual dinner to celebrate the achievements and a few big wigs will be attending."

"When is dinner?"

Clicking through emails, a post about Videl's funeral went around the office. "In a month."

"Perfect opportunity for us to mingle."

"Okay. Thanks, Nicco."

"For?"

I felt bashful under his gaze. "Not turning your back on me."

"If nothing else, you have me."

Those words felt heartfelt. "My parents are going to freak out."

"It is best to not let them know what's really going on."

I felt awkward at my next question. "What is your last name?"

He swept his arms up and chortled. "Kind of late for that, but Montoya."

"Nicco Montoya. I like it."

"I like Charlie Amor."

A knock at the door interrupted us, and my secretary, Yvonne, arrived with my morning coffee and workload.

Yvonne reached out to hand me the drink. "I thought you could use a strong one today."

"Thanks. Are they still downstairs talking?" I took a sip of the Americano latte.

"A few people scattered back to their office. Hi, I'm Yvonne."

"Nicco."

"Sorry, Yvonne. Nicco is my boyfriend," I said to her and introduced him.

"Nice to meet you, Nicco. Would you like a coffee from the employee lounge?" Yvonne offered.

Nicco rubbed his chin. "No, actually I'm leaving for work myself."

"Oh, what do you do?" Yvonne interrogated.

"Banking. Garbage pickup," Nicco and I answered at the same time.

Yvonne held a perplexed look.

"He works for a company that handles garbage pickup for banks," I lied, not wanting to give his real job of being in security and tipping everybody off.

"Okay, well Nicco, again, nice to meet you." Yvonne left my office and I sat back in my seat, heaving a long sigh out.

Nicco folded his arms. "Our stories need to sync up."

"You are right. Tonight we can go through the basic details."

"A night out would help you relax."

"Like a date?"

Nicco leaned over my desk. "If you want to call it that."

"How would that work? I mean, shouldn't we stay inside?"

Nicco waved his hand around my office. "Charlie, relax. You're already out in the world. Hector won't make a move so fast after killing Videl."

"Maybe you're right. I get nervous and jumpy about anything to do with the Torrio family now."

He stretched his arm to cover my hand and squeezed. "I understand, but I promise he won't hurt you on my watch."

I smiled. "Thanks again, Nicco."

"Let me head out so you can get to work. Call me when you're ready to leave."

"I will."

Winking at me, he left my office, keeping the door open. I ran through the new proposals on my desk and logged in the new land and housing itemized for demolition. After two hours of reading through everything, I removed my glasses, stretched, and stood out of my seat. I grabbed my usual mug and left the office to get a refill. I walked past and heard whispering near the bathrooms.

"What are you talking about?"

"If she knows anything that can be a problem."

"She wouldn't do anything to us, besides, we have her place bugged."

I crouched against the wall, listening intently.

"Charlie." A voice startled me.

"Hey, Craig." I nervously stood up.

"Everything alright, you look flushed," Craig said.

Hearing footsteps leave, I walked further into the hallway near the bathroom, but no one was there.

"Sorry. Yeah, fine."

His voice made my spine stiffen with emotions. "Tough about Videl."

"Still hard to believe." I continued to the lounge, refilled my cup, and picked up a donut.

Craig opened the fridge and grabbed milk for his coffee.

"Are you going to the funeral?"

"No, stuff like that makes me uneasy."

"Charlie." The hairs on the back of my neck stood up at the sound of his voice.

Spilling some of my coffee on the counter, I flustered at him finding me. "Ye-Yeah," I stammered.

"Come to my office," Hector commanded.

"Is something wrong?"

"In my office," Hector demanded. Craig looked away and I sauntered out of the lounge, feeling my pocket for the pen Nicco gave me.

Hector gestured for me to take a seat on the couch. I glanced around his office. Nothing stood out and I wondered if he left any evidence about Videl's death.

Turning the locks, he licked his lips and stalked over to the couch and took a seat across from me, planting his hand on my thigh.

"How are you feeling?"

I scooted back, placing my cup down to face him. "Doing as well as can be expected."

The glare in his eyes from me backing up wasn't missed. "I care about you, Charlie."

"As the Chief Designer, I know you care about all of your employees."

"True, but I think we've gotten closer over the past few years."

"We're co-workers."

"For now."

"Hector."

"Listen, I know you're getting spooked by what happened to Videl, but I can protect you."

I stared at him. "How?"

"Come to the annual dinner with me, and we can talk further."

"My boyfriend is coming with me." I picked up the cup. He slipped a hand back on my thigh and I jumped back, spilling it on his shirt and pants.

"Fuck!" Hector yelled, wiping his pants down.

I covered my mouth in shock and reached for tissues off his table. "I am so sorry. You're right. I'm really jumpy today." I moved my hand inside my pocket to grab the pen to turn it on.

Hector walked into his bathroom. "Not your fault. Maybe some time off would help."

I softly walked to his desk, touched his mouse, and searched through his emails and files. "I love to work. Being here helps take off the stress."

"If you think it's best."

Forwarding some of his papers to myself and emails that said urgent, I clicked out of his computer and shuffled back to stand against the couch.

He came out of the bathroom right at that moment, smiling at me. "Let me take you out tonight, a nice meal and drinks."

I moved out of his hold. "Hector, you know I have a boyfriend."

"Mighty funny he popped up today," he grunted, narrowing his eyes.

"What are you saying?"

"Saying you've never talked about him until today. How many times have I asked you out?"

I groaned, throwing my hands in the air. "Are you really asking me that right now?"

"I'm owed an explanation."

I pointed at his chest. "I don't owe you a damn thing. You are the CEO, but I work for your father."

He held his hands up in surrender. "Sorry, Charlie. There's something about you I like and want to protect."

"Protection from what?"

"People that want to fill your head with lies about me." He stepped closer to me. Ready for the day to be over, I reached for the cup again and swiveled around him to leave. "Keep me updated on the annual dinner, and I will get the new designs sent by later in the week."

Chapter 5

Nicco

It was still early in the day, and the sun was shining when I left Charlie at work. The day consisted of us running Hector's phone records, along with his father's and associates. Now that I had an entry through Charlie, making contact in person would be smooth sailing to grab them both up.

"Are you ready?" I spoke in the earpiece to my team.

"Check. Locked on target," Knox answered. A few of us came to the strip club that Hector was partial owner of where some deals were being handled. The police were called in to assist. We expected the news to pick it up, but not much would dent his organization.

"Three in the back. Keep an eye out in the alley," I announced and motioned to go ahead.

It was only three in the afternoon. Not too many people would be here, but showing our presence would bring Hector out to make mistakes.

"Arghhhhh!!" Some women were screaming. Guys tried to run. I pointed the gun, giving out commands.

"Stop, or you will end up in jail so fast, your head will spin."

A few tears streamed down their faces. "We got activity, Boss!" Wesley shouted from the back room.

Nasir and I marched to the back, allowing the police to handle the front. I kept my gun raised, ready for anything to jump out.

Shoving the door open, Wesley moved to the barrels on the side of the wall and we saw four men sitting at the table.

"Did we miss all the fun?" I taunted, lifting the tops off the barrels, seeing guns and drums stacked together.

"There's at least a million or five about to be sold," Nasir remarked.

"Chump change for him," I answered.

"Who are you?" one of the guys asked.

I sneered, landing on his face. "Where's the boss?"

"You're talking to him," he scoffed.

"The Torrio Mafia is behind this club, drugs, and guns. Save yourself and get fewer years in jail if you tell us the truth."

"Fuck you!" he spat, trying to get out of the chair. All four of them were handcuffed behind their backs.

"Hector has you all fooled. I'm giving you a chance to save yourselves." I picked up the cocaine and tossed it on top of the table.

"Not mine," the short, bald gentleman spat.

All three of the other men glared at him. "Seems your friends would rather take the fall for Hector."

"I manage the club only," he spoke.

"Shut the fuck up!" the spiked hair man yelled, blood dripping down his nose.

"Take them out. I will get the rest of their statements later."

Wesley and the team walked them out through the lobby and outside to squad cars.

"Hector is either slipping or someone is trying to make us think he's the leader," Nasir commented.

Capping the lid on the barrel, I watched the men tag everything and load up. I went to the front of the strip club, then to the back offices. I noticed some of the women getting dressed as the police put them in handcuffs.

"Where's the manager's office?" I questioned.

"Three doors down the hall," one of the women, who avoided making eye contact, answered slowly.

"Thanks."

Nasir and I marched in, keeping the door open while the team continued mobilizing the stash of guns and drugs. Searching through drawers, cabinets, scanning files, nothing stood out, which gave me an idea that Hector was smarter than I expected.

"Anything on your end?" I lifted my head to glance at Nasir sitting at the desk.

"Simple orders for liquor, and schedules for the dancers."

Closing the file cabinet, I stood off to the side. "We should get a trace on his computer."

"Wesley will start today," Nasir answered, speaking into the earpiece.

"Let's head out. Time for me to pick up Charlie."

"How is that going?" Half of the team left out behind me, and I checked the time, seeing I had fifteen minutes to get back to her office.

"Fine."

Opening the door, I slid into the driver's side. Nasir stood next to me with the keys in his hand ready to slide off to car behind me.

"Remember it's only pretend." He grinned.

I started the ignition. "What are you getting at?"

Shrugging me off, he. "We all have those moments if we're doing it just for a case, or if she's really becoming your woman."

I waved him off. "Not on my mind at all."

"Not yet."

Chortling at his response, we left the club, going back in the opposite direction to make it in time for her to be off. Right as I pulled up, I hopped out and walked down a block to report in with Chapel, one of the surveillance crew. Shaking hands with him, I leaned into the window and watched the office as people came and went through the building.

"How was today?"

"Quiet." Chapel answered.

Dragged a hand down my face. "Anything stand out?"

Chapel picked up his notepad. "No. Hector did leave about an hour ago."

"Sure it was to go check in on what happened at the club."

"Possibly. A limo arrived and he hopped inside with a guy and girl."

"You get pictures?"

"It was too fast. We did get the license plate though," Chapel answered.

"Cool. Send them to me and get everything over to Aydin to sync with Wesley."

Chapel put his car in drive. I noticed Charlie sauntering out of the office talking with a guy. "On top of it, boss. Are we following you and the lady home?"

"The second shift should be at my place by now. You can head out." Dapping, I walked to the car and opened the door for her, taking her bag out of her hand.

"How was your day, babe?" I caught a smile across her face, and the guy backed up.

"It was good. Nicco, this is my co-worker, Craig," Charlie introduced us.

Ignoring his hand, I motioned for Charlie to get in the car. "Craig, is it?"

He scratched his forehead. "Yeah, I work in the same department as Charlie."

"Good to know. How long have you been crushing on her?" I pointed at the car.

"What?!" Craig's confused reaction to my question only gave me the sign that Charlie had almost every person at the company interested in her for the right or wrong reasons.

"She's spoken for." I explained.

Charlie threw her hands up in frustration. "Nicco, Craig's just a co-worker," Charlie quipped.

"As long as he knows you're taken."

Charlie motioned between us. "Taken? This is all pretend."

"What do you want to eat tonight?" I ignored her statement and went home.

* * *

Shoving her coat and purse down on the couch and the aggravated stare on her face were the first signs I could recognize that I pissed her off. Charlie was different from what I was used to in women. She's calm, confident, smart, and sweet. The idea to pretend we were in a relationship came out of selfish reasons, but I would never put her in harm's way over a crush. The moment we met, I felt a strong attraction. Even going to her place to arrest her for working with Hector, over the conversation she came across as innocent and scared.

"Did you find anything at work today?" Removing the items for making tacos, I settled in the kitchen, prepping while she glared at me.

"Can you explain what happened back there?"

"No."

The retort sprang to her lips of its own accord. "No, you won't explain?"

"I can see a snake a mile away, Charlie."

"Craig's harmless." She forced a demure smile.

I hiked up my left brow from cutting the tomatoes. "Take my word for it. He's trouble."

Charlie stole a piece of tomato from the counter. "I guess I have to get used to having bodyguards all day."

"Better to let us weed out the snakes."

"Hector's the big snake. What do you think Criag is doing?"

"Too early to tell, but it will reveal itself."

"I guess. Today he kind of interrupted me when I was spying on a conversation."

"What conversation?"

"Not sure if I understood what they were talking about, but it sounded like it was about me."

"Tell me." I poured the meat in the pan while she grabbed the plates from the cabinet and salsa from the fridge.

"Basically, they said something in the vein of, *if she knows anything, that can be a problem.*"

"You have no idea who was talking?"

"No and that scares me. They were whispering low."

Ambling to the stove, Charlie took out two glasses and grabbed the utensils. "Did you get the pen in his office?"

Charlie sprinted to the living room and came back to the kitchen. She turned it on, hearing Hector's voice.

"Annual dinner in a month."

I trailed behind her to the living room, and we sat beside each other. "Anything you can share with me from today?" Charlie quizzed.

"My team and I busted a strip club that Hector partially owns."

Her voice was hard as steel. "I knew he had hands in a lot of underground businesses."

"A few pounds of cocaine and guns."

She reached down to remove her shoes. "Can that stick for him to get arrested?"

"He has access to the best lawyers. He could have the charges thrown out."

"I feel like I need to do more."

"Going in and acting normal is all you need to do."

Her eyes softened a little. "Tomorrow I have to visit one of the sites they plan on building."

"What time?"

"About nine and then I planned to meet up with my friends for drinks."

"Perfect timing. I can drive you and you can plant some surprises for Hector."

"Does your girlfriend mind you having me here?"

If she only knew I planned on her being my one and only girlfriend. "Girlfriend?" I chuckled.

"Am I wrong? You're handsome and have a career that you love. I'm surprised you haven't been locked down."

"My career is my girlfriend."

Charlie popped the bottle open and stared at me. "So, you are not dating anyone?"

I dropped the napkin on the table, clasped my hands together, and leaned forward. "Ask me what you want to really know, Charlie."

Shrugging her shoulders, she gulped her drink. "I find it hard to believe no woman has come and knocked on your door or called."

"For one thing, I know how to keep my private life from business."

She looked off at my answer. "Right, business."

"Since Hector's not your type, then who is the lucky man for Charlie?"

She exhaled a long breath. "My dating life has been non-existent for a while."

Taking my plate and gesturing for hers, I stood up. "I can clean the dishes since you cooked," Charlie said.

I answered, "You can help. I don't mind."

"Okay, like I was saying. Same as you. Work has consumed me for the past few months and year."

Turning on the faucet, I cleaned the remaining food into the trash. "What would be your ideal date?"

Narrowing her eyes, she tapped a finger to her cheek. "A walk."

"Huh?" My brows bunched together in surprise.

"A walk, maybe coffee, and we just talk."

"Most women say dinner, movie, or large setting in public."

"I am not like most women."

Our eyes connected for a minute, then got interrupted

by the ringing of my phone. I stepped back, reached for my cell, leaving her to finish washing and heading to my office.

"Yeah."

"I figured you'd want to know any updates," Wesley quipped.

Shutting the door behind me, I stood in front of my desk.

"Good news and bad news."

"Tell me the bad first."

"Voice recording won't be any good to nail Hector. We need something heavier."

"I estimated."

"Good news is the license plate from the limo came back to being owned by Izan Torrio and the camera footage from the building showed Hector and Charlie's assistant leaving together."

"Her assistant Yvonne?"

Wesley responded, "Same thing I said."

"Get me everything on Yvonne and track Elaine the receptionist."

"Who's Elaine?" Wesley asked.

"Main office receptionist. I guess she knows a lot of secrets at the company."

"Right on it, man."

"Thanks."

"Aye, you know if Charlie's dating anybody?" Wesley questioned.

"Motherfucker!" I barked.

He burst into laughter and I heard more chuckling in the background. "Fuck off my line."

"See you tomorrow, man," Wesley taunted and hung up.

Seeing Charlie poke her head inside, I sat back in thought. "Do you have some news?" she asked.

Debating if I wanted to give too much away and have her nervous around the people she worked with, I pushed the phone in my pocket and stood. "Still running reports. You want to catch a movie before you head to bed?"

"Sure, but I get to pick tonight."

"Why?"

"Because your entire Netflix is filled with bounty hunters and Nicolas Cage movies," Charlie joked, and I playfully bumped her in the shoulder.

Watching her bend over to look at the movie selection in the cabinet, I licked my lips at her shapely figure. Having thoughts was fine, but moving on them could hurt the case and I'm determined to get Hector Torrio before he comes for her.

Getting comfortable on the couch, she pushed the covers over her legs and sat next to me. I stretched my arm across the back of the couch, and she leaned her head on my shoulder to be more comfortable, causing her scent to fill my nose.

"What perfume are you wearing?"

"Rose petals by a designer I found locally. Is it too strong?" She smelled her hand and glanced up at me. I was mesmerized by her lips before moving up to her eyes as she caught me staring.

"Not strong. I actually think you should wear it more often." I slid some of her hair out of her face.

A lump formed in her throat as she caught her breath. "Okay, thanks."

Chapter 6

Charlie

My morning consisted of me apologizing to Nicco for practically falling asleep in his lap. Somehow, we'd found ourselves caught together dozing off after the second movie played. I guess the past few days finally got to me because I barely felt like I was in the zone of everything in my life. A movie playing before my eyes and I couldn't yell cut. Nicco hadn't spoken a word since we got in the car and stopped for breakfast. Almost at work, I hesitated on bringing up last night. The feeling of his arms around me, stiff girth poking my stomach, made me think of my college days.

"Today shouldn't take long," I said.

He nodded, a sardonic smile gleamed in his eyes.

"If you want, I can take an uber or get my friend to pick me up, so you head to work."

"Why would I do that?"

Our eyes met. "I mean you seem so grouchy today."

Nicco sighed. "I'm fine, Charlie."

"Are you sure? If you're tired of me, I can sleep at my parents' place or get a hotel." My heart fluttered wildly.

A vein throbbed on his forehead. "Did I say I was tired of you?"

"No."

"There's your answer."

I mumbled under my breath, "You haven't talked to me."

"Huh?" He arrived and parked next to the other cars from the company.

I blew out a breath. "Are you mad at me?"

"Should I be?"

"Answer my question first."

We'd quickly made a connection and pushing me away because of Hector was not what I wanted. "What is your question?"

"Very childish, Nicco." I reached for the door, and he grasped my arm.

"Close the door."

The look in his eyes told me I should obey. The other part of me hated to be told what to do. "Or what?"

He smirked, licking his lips. "Charlie, please close the door."

Feeling like I won the first battle, I shut the door and turned to face him with my arms crossed off. "Go ahead."

"I can tell you grew up spoiled."

"Shut up," I giggled, and he laughed.

"I like you," he blurted out.

"Oh."

"Yeah, and right now running the lead on the Torrio case means I shouldn't be distracted."

It stung a little bit at his revelation of me being a distraction, but I understood for safety reasons.

"I never want to be a distraction for you, so maybe I

should go stay with a friend and put somebody else as my guard," I suggested.

He shook his head with a scowl on his face. "Never going to happen."

"Can we talk about him later? The team is looking over at the car. Maybe I should go." I pointed at Hector and a few of his men.

Growling at Hector, Nicco nodded. I climbed out of the car, gripping the plans I drew up, and headed to the group of my workers. "Morning, Charlie," Craig, the crew lead, smiled at me.

"Morning, Craig. How is everything looking?"

He scratched his head. "So far we got the plans lined up to break ground on schedule."

Hector clapped him on the back. "Charlie, you know Craig proposed we put an extra four thousand square feet to open up more retail space."

"Interesting."

Craig looked surprised at Hector's statement. Both men looked off, and I turned around to see Nicco approaching us. "Babe, you forgot your purse." Nicco arrived, pressing a kiss on my forehead.

"Thanks. My mind is still foggy."

"Charlie, you know we keep our properties free of outsiders," Hector informed me.

"Well good thing I'm not an outsider and her boyfriend," Nicco challenged, staring at Hector.

Hector chuckled at his glare. "A boyfriend that won't last."

"Is that a threat?" Nicco walked up on Hector.

I jumped in the middle to separate them and placed my hand on Nicco's chest. "Nicco, this is my place of business."

"Listen to your girlfriend," Hector taunted.

"Hector, I came here to work, not to break up a fight over nonsense."

Nodding, we started back on work, reading through the documents and setting up details for Craig and his team to get started. After about a few hours of running through information, I replied to messages to go eat with my friends.,

* * *

After washing her hands, Dedra wiped the counter down, then took a seat on the patio next to me and her cousin, Paula.

"Any news on Videl's murder?" Dedra filled our cups with water and lemon.

"I know the funeral happened. Some people went."

Paula took a bite of her sandwich. "You actually saw his dead body?"

"Something I really don't want to talk about anymore."

"Yeah, let's talk about the fine ass man bodyguarding you and you living with him," Dedra mentioned.

My eyes jumped wide. "Dedra," I groaned.

"What did I miss?" Paula motioned between me and Dedra.

Dedra giggled. "Tell her or I will."

"Nothing, Paula."

Dedra huffed. "Some sexy guys burst into her place thinking she's the enemy and Charlie ends up with a boyfriend."

I rolled my eyes. "We're talking about somebody that died, Dedra."

"Videl worked with you and I sent prayers to his family, but come on! Your life at the moment is like a Lifetime movie however you look at it, and you might as well have sex with the hot guy," Dedra determined.

Paula laughed and I couldn't help but join in at Dedra with her dramatic comments. "No one is having sex."

"Tell us the truth. If he initiated, would you do it?" Dedra wondered.

"So today I went to work and Hector was there, acting pretentious again. Nicco almost got in his face." I ignored her question.

"Hector's full of himself. You should stay far away from him." Dedra devoured her salad.

I blew out a breath. "I wish I could, but they've gotten me deep into a situation I doubt I could get out of right now."

"How so?"

"I think they framed me to take the fall for embezzlement."

Silence spread and both looked at me with sadness in their eyes. "You have to go to the police, Charlie," Paula begged.

"I tried, but Nicco thinks it best to work another angle."

"Nicco might be right, but is he going to testify for you when the police come knocking at your door?" Dedra fussed.

I released a long exhale. "At the moment, he's all I got on my side to go up against Hector."

"Have you spoken to your parents? How are they?"

"My mom called me a few days ago and I promised to come by and spend time with them, but I hate to drag them into my mess."

"Ignoring their calls won't help," Paula said, giving me some things to think about.

Checking the time on my watch, I saw it was getting late and I needed to run by the grocery store to make dinner for Nicco as a thank you.

"Ladies, thanks for letting me vent this afternoon. My life has been chaotic lately and having you two has helped." I stood and picked up my purse.

"Are you leaving already?" Paula remarked.

"I am. I wanted to surprise Nicco with dinner tonight. He's always cooking for me." I shrugged.

"Sounds like wifey material," Dedra instigated.

Waving her off, I bent down to hug Paula, then Dedra. I walked off to the front of the house and saw a car detail sitting out front that Nicco told me about when he had to leave in a rush.

"Hi guys. Can I run by the store to grab some things for dinner?"

Starting the car, both gentlemen nodded and unlocked the door, letting me slip in the backseat. Dedra and Paula had me thinking of my parents and I decided to give them a call, while it's fresh on my mind.

"Hello."

"Charlie, my angel," Dad answered.

I smiled. "Hi, Dad."

"Hi, pumpkin. Why haven't we seen you, young lady?"

I could hear the frown in his voice. "Work has kept me busy."

"Is that Charlie?" Mom yelled.

"You hear your mother?" Dad jokes.

"Tell her I said hello."

"She says hello, dear," Dad replied.

The car arrived at the market a few minutes later. I hopped out. One guard escorted me inside and grabbed a basket.

"What's all that noise?" Dad investigated.

Nicco would be surprised at me cooking tonight. "I'm at the grocery store."

"We heard about some guy that works at your job getting killed."

Having to explain to my folks all the ins and outs of what has gone on would have them both worried and stressed.

I pulled a bag of fruit and added fresh veggies to my cart. "Unfortunately, I shouldn't really talk about it, Dad. How are you and Mom?"

"I'll let you get away with changing the subject this one time, but we're good."

I tittered. "Sorry."

Dad exhaled. "You're our baby, so we worry."

"I know, Dad, but I promise when I have more to tell I will let you know, but there's something else."

"What?" he asked.

"I have a boyfriend."

He raised his voice in concern. "Who is this guy and has your mother met him before?"

"No."

"Well, he needs to come and meet us as soon as possible," Dad announced.

"In due time."

"We have the weekend free, so that makes it perfect timing," Dad insisted.

I groaned and stomped my feet like a kid. "Daddy."

"The more you keep from us, Charlie, the longer we worry."

"Listen to your father, Charlie," my mom yelled in the background.

"Alright, I will ask and see what he says."

"Tell him your father insists on meeting him if wants to keep seeing my angel."

I laughed, putting the groceries on the register to pay. "Okay, old man. Talk to you soon."

We bagged up the groceries and headed to the car. As we climbed back inside, I noticed the same car from my place the night Videl was killed. Shaking off my thoughts, I got in and stared at my phone, curious if Nicco was thinking about me. Traffic, unlike earlier in the day, was smooth getting back to his place. The guards offered to help bring in the groceries and I declined. Turning to shut the door, I noticed that same car two blocks up from Nicco's place.

"Can you get Nicco on the phone?" I muttered.

"Is something wrong?"

"I don't know, but I have a bad feeling."

"He's out on an emergency run," the bodyguard mentioned.

"I might be crazy for my thoughts, but the car parked down the block looks familiar." Soon as the words came out of my mouth the car started up and drove past us speeding down the street.

"Did you get the license plate?" he asked.

"No, I saw the same car at the grocery store."

"Nicco will help us, but maybe we should take her to the office," the shorter guy with tattoos, named Six, said.

Checking the time on my watch, my plans to cook him dinner went out the window when I saw that car. "He's right. Drop the food off and hop back in the car." He held the door open for me and I sprinted to the building, put the groceries away, and came back down in ten minutes to leave again.

Chapter 7

Nicco

Hearing from Gary and Six that someone possibly followed them with Charlie in the car sent a signal to my brain that Hector was getting more dangerous by the minute. When I left Charlie earlier with her friends, the emergency came through the wire of Hector's father at a closed off meeting with a few higher people in Mayor's office. Having the backing of senators and council members could easily get the Torrio Mafia into more doors and being untouchable. Waiting for the sun to go down and come here at night worked out for the best, less eyes trying to block anything. I sat in the backseat wanting to charge in and take them all down, but it would work out better for us to have more evidence on them. I knew she felt on edge and wanted me to stick around, but passing this opportunity into someone else's hands made me nervous. I sat up in the seat watching Izan and Hector come out of the building, talking and walking together heading to their car.

"Stay on them."

"You know following the car might spook them," Wesley mentioned.

"Doesn't matter. I want him to know we're coming."

Pulling a few cars behind, their limo left in the direction I assumed was back to the company building and I was right. Both men, alongside their guards, walked in past security and I dialed Charlie's number.

"Nicco," Charlie whispered.

"Is there a way to get past security in your office building?"

"Uhm, maybe through the security shift change," Charlie suggested.

"What time does that happen?"

"Around right about now," Charlie responded, looking down at the clock on the radio going on seven fifty-five.

"Stick by your phone."

"What are you planning on doing?"

"Breaking in to confront Hector."

She gasped. "Nicco, wait, you can't."

"Trust me."

"I do, but Hector's too powerful."

"He thinks he's powerful, but he's hiding behind his father's money."

"What about the annual dinner?"

"Still on track. I just want to see what they're up to right now."

"Please be careful."

"I will." I hung up, easing out of the car with Nasir as the lookout, and sprinted to the side of the building. I noticed a guard on a smoke break. Tossing my head in his direction, Nasir understood to look as backup and I rushed over and tapped him on the shoulder.

"Aye, you got a light?" I asked.

"Nobody—"

Before he could answer, I punched him in the face, knocking him out and then dragging him to the alleyway. I changed into his clothes, while Nasir restrained his hands and mouth with a rag. I marched around the corner, going in and walking right past security with my head down.

"Barney, you came back quick!" another guard shouted, assuming I was the guard. I gestured with my hat. Climbing on the elevator, I remembered the floor for Hector's office. I kept my head down, away from the cameras. Nasir spoke in the earpiece, but the static cut in and out.

Stepping out of the elevator, I stalked down the hall and heard loud yelling.

"A screw up is a screw up Hector!" Izan fussed.

"She doesn't know anything about the business."

"Charlie is smart and will figure it out!" Izan shouted.

I stood outside the open door, ear against the wall.

"Our plans are running fine. The more we can get attached to her name, the better the outcome."

"Videl's death has bitten us in the ass. The police are snooping around more," Izan hissed.

"Pay them off," Hector emphasized.

"My hands are tied. You caused a pile up and you need to fix it or else."

"Both of us want the same things—more money and power."

"I built the Torrio organization. I refuse to let you burn it down." Izan grimaced.

"I can control Charlie."

"Who is the guy she's saying is her boyfriend?"

Slowly, I eased my head around to peek through the door. Hector and his father stood nose to nose at the side of the window.

"Some idiot named Nicco."

"Find out about him. Maybe we could use him to our advantage."

"She can do better."

Izan chuckled. "Like you?"

"What's wrong with me and her dating?"

"Charlie's too good for you," Izan remarked, raising a hand in the air.

"Either she marries me or goes to jail for embezzlement."

"Blackmail," Izan hissed. Hector paused and turned his head.

"What other choice does she have? I will save her, and she will be grateful."

"You are delusional, son. Charlie will never want to be with you. Stick to the plan and move the money out before it's too late," Izan demanded, turning to leave. I jogged out of view into the corner of the hallway, watching him hop on the elevator. Hector was still in his office. I waited a few minutes before leaving and catching up to the team outside. I scanned my surrounding, climbed in the car.

"Izan came down and left. Is Hector still upstairs?" Nasir questioned.

"Yeah, his plan is to blackmail Charlie." I removed the hat and jacket. Wesley turned the ignition and left the building.

"We knew he was planning something," Nasir said and typed on his phone.

"He wants Charlie and besides putting her name on

those documents for embezzlement, I think he would give it up to keep her for himself."

"And risk his father's anger?" Nasir quizzed.

"He would, because he's obsessed with her."

"Damn," Wesley muttered.

Parking back at TN Security, the door opened and Charlie rushed out and ran into my arms. I squeezed her tightly, brushing a hand down her back.

"I was scared," Charlie mumbled.

I smiled. "Nothing to be afraid of Charlie."

"Hector's dangerous."

"Come on. We can head to my place and talk."

"What did you find out?" Charlie circled her arm in mine.

I kissed her on the forehead. "Relax. Hector's not a threat unless you let him be one."

The screeching of a car speeding down the road had Charlie halting. I pushed her down on the ground and motioned for Nasir and Wesley. I watched the car coming faster down the road. I got in position with my gun as bullets came out of the back window.

"Nicco!" Charlie screamed. I focused on the car until it left.

"Stay down!" I yelled, running toward the vehicle, hearing more of my team coming out of the building.

"The police are called," Aydin said, standing next to me.

Catching my breath, the car disappeared into the night until I only saw the taillights fade away.

* * *

Slamming the door at the office, all eyes mirrored the emotions shining in mine— aggravation, anger, disappointment for letting someone get close enough to take a shot when we knew how dangerous it could get. Aydin wiped a hand down his face, seething as he scanned over the details from the police report.

"We know tonight was a message from the Torrio family."

"How sure are you?" Knox commented.

"No other case is high profile, and Charlie being seen with me might have tipped him off. We're not naive enough to think he didn't do a check up on me."

"Maybe Charlie should have other arrangements for protection," Carlos recommended, and my fists balled up, knowing having someone else protect her wouldn't work.

"The look in your eyes tells me you hate my suggestion, but you're too close to the subject," Carlos hammered in.

"Carlos might have a point, but Charlie's already familiar with Nicco," Aydin backed me up.

Throwing his hands up, Carlos sat back and listened.

"A direct hit on Charlie tonight means Hector's feeling the heat."

"Take the proof you do have to the DA and see what happens," Nasir insisted.

"We can try, but we know after the meeting his father and him had with the police commissioner it might not work," I claimed.

"Where's Charlie right now?" Nasir quizzed.

"Sitting with Molly in my office," I replied.

"From now on we will double up protection. We need to be aware the Governor could be in their back pockets," Aydin suggested.

"I'm almost close to finding out the driver that Hector uses," Wesley hinted.

"Bring him in for questioning."

"Why not go to him instead, especially if we make him think Hector sent us." I smirked.

Aydin leaned on the back of the chair. "Keep talking."

"Hector hates disloyalty, make him paranoid about his people and he crumbles."

Nasir and Aydin gleamed at each other.

"Try that angle and move forward if he breaks," Aydin explained.

"Then let me get Charlie out of here. I know she's still upset about tonight."

"Take her to a hotel for the night. Going right back to your place is too much for her."

I nodded my head. "Thanks. Keep me updated on when you move on his driver."

"Take care of Charlie first." Aydin stuck his hand out.

Opening the door, I passed down the hall and sighed. I was ready to take care of Hector, but the time wasn't right now. He'd made it known I'm a problem for him and I was the right guy to answer.

Charlie would never be his victim.

Slipping my hand around the knob, I slowly tapped and waited for permission to enter. A soft voice said, "It's open." Seeing Charlie wrapped in a blanket with her eyes closed, lying on the couch had me in possessive mode. I had to keep her safe at all costs.

"She's been asleep for the last thirty minutes," Molly whispered.

"Is she upset?"

"A little, but more so because of you."

"Me?"

Molly drew a hand across her forehead. "She thought you got hurt."

"We're used to this type of action."

She patted me on the arm. "She's not, and she cares about you."

"You think she wants out?" Knowing Charlie wanted out would hurt, but I understood my lifestyle could be difficult to navigate.

Molly stood from the chair. "I can't answer that for her."

Stretching my arms, I scratched the back of my neck. "Thanks, Molly. Let me get her to the hotel for the night."

"Try not to worry, Nicco. She likes you a lot."

I removed my vibrating phone from my pocket and ignored a text from my brother. "I fucked up tonight."

"Beating yourself up will never help. Everyone is safe."

I twisted my lip up. I was pissed off. "My case and I almost got her killed."

"Charlie's here and safe. At the end of the day your job is to protect her and you did. Now go and get her out of here. I told her about meeting the girls tomorrow."

"Amelia and Cyrah."

"Yep, I think it might help," Molly answered. I strolled over to Charlie, running a hand up her arm, and shook her awake.

Molly grabbed her purse and coat.

"Nicco," Charlie mumbled.

"Yeah, it's me. I'm going to take you to a hotel for the night."

"What time is it?" Charlie queried.

I raised my wrist and looked at my watch. "Almost two a.m."

"I have to work tomorrow," Charlie groaned.

"Take the day off."

Charlie threw the blanket back and stood up. "That will look weird if I don't show up for work."

"She's right, Nicco," Molly agreed.

"Let's get you in bed for right now." Pressing a kiss to her forehead, I took her by the hand and walked out of the office to my car. She climbed in and I shut the door for her. She leaned her head back against the seat and closed her eyes.

"I thought you got hurt tonight." Charlie drew a deep, audible breath.

I started the car, and I turned to look at her. "Never worry about me."

She smiled softly. "Too late."

Leaning over the armrest, I stared into her eyes. I cupped her chin and covered her lips with mine.

Her hair was disheveled. I pushed it behind her ear. "Mmmmm..." Charlie moaned, sucking on my tongue. Before we got carried away, I pulled back.

"Tomorrow, Molly wants you to meet the other wives." Driving away from the office, I turned my lights on and scanned around the block to make sure we weren't followed.

"She told me Amelia is married to Aydin and Cyrah is Nasir's wife."

"I think you will like the girls."

She rested her hand on the back of my neck. "Amelia works at the company, right?"

I chuckled at how Amelia and Aydin used to act with each other. "Yeah."

"Why are you laughing?"

"Thinking of how Amelia and Aydin started out."

"What do you mean?'

I motioned between us. "Similar to you and me."

I cuffed my right hand. "In what way?"

"He was assigned to protect her and they ended up getting married."

Charlie's mouth opened and closed in shock. "Ohh."

Finally arriving at the hotel, I parked and helped Charlie out. I held her hand and placed the other on my hip close to my gun.

"Why did we come here?" Charlie wondered.

"Safer for right now to let things clear out."

"I don't have any clothes."

"Tomorrow we'll get you some clothes. We're here just for tonight." After slipping the clerk my credit card to pay, I escorted Charlie to the elevator and to our suite, I let her pick which room she wanted to sleep in and I took the couch for the night on high alert.

Chapter 8

Charlie

Being back at work seemed weird and I felt a little paranoid that people knew about the shooting. Checking over my new reports, I hesitated to even leave my office, but Hector would probably think it's suspicious if I didn't come to the meeting tonight. Every other week they gathered the heads of each department to run down the new proposals, and I planned on trying to get more information out of him to help Nicco in his quest to get Hector locked up. Rising out of my chair, I grabbed all of my designs I was asked to create. Leaving my office, I waved at Craig and Yvonne who were flirting with each other.

"Do you need me in the meeting with you, Charlie?" Yvonne asked.

"No, I'll be fine."

"I have your lunch order already," Yvonne announced.

"Thanks, girl." I sauntered down the hall, exhaled a breath and put on a fake smile as I shoved the conference room door open.

"Charlie, good to see this morning," Izan Torrio said, and I gulped down the knot in my throat, never expecting him to show up to the office.

"Where is everyone?"

"I asked everyone to continue working. I only need you today," Hector expressed, and he motioned for me to take a seat.

"Okay. Is there something wrong?"

"No, of course not."

I pulled out my chair, laid my things on the table, sat down, and scooted in my chair.

"Charlie, you've been working for the company a long time," Izan explained.

"Thank you, Mr. Torrio."

Hector's cold eyes studied me. "With that in mind, we've been thinking about next steps."

"Next steps?" My brow hiked, curious where the conversation was going.

Hector got up and came around the table, placing his hands on the back of the chair. "My father is trying to say that we want you to head the company."

"Excuse me?"

"Don't scare the poor girl," Izan chuckled.

"The construction part, of course. I will be here to help guide you and work closely together, but you becoming CEO of Torrio Construction is a perfect opportunity, Charlie." Hector planted his hands on my shoulders, giving me a massage.

"You have to relax, Charlie. I can feel the knots in your shoulders," Hector laughed.

I smiled. "Honestly, I don't know what to say. I mean, I'm grateful you considered me."

He waved his hand. "Think about what it would do

for your career. You don't have to answer today. Take some time. We have the big dinner in a few days, and you can give an answer then." Izan smiled.

"What about you, Hector?"

"My father and I talked, and we both think you would be a great choice as the face of the company."

"The right face of the company," I repeated.

Hector grinned. "Are those the new designs?"

"They are."

"I can check them out and get any changes to you later today."

"Sure, and Hector I wanted to ask you a personal question."

He waited for my response. "Ask away." His eyes swept up and down my body.

Revealing my thoughts might make him think something is deeper, but to help Nicco with his case, I needed to nail down more information. "Are you dating Elaine?"

"The receptionist?"

I could sense a lie was about to come from him. "Yes."

"Are you jealous?" He licked his lips and stared at me.

"Hector."

He slipped his finger around a loose curl in my hair. "Me and Elaine fooled around a few times. Why?"

"I heard her talking about you two having dinner last night." I made up the lie on the spot to see if he'd give away his whereabouts.

"Dinner is the last thing I would do with Elaine."

"I figured. I mean you've always hinted at us dating and now you move in on another person at the office?" I giggled, flirting in the moment to see how far he'd go in his lies.

"Only person I would give the world to is you, Charlie."

"Okay, Loverboy." I reached to grab the door and he slipped a hand around my wrist.

"I am serious, Charlie. Drop that fake boyfriend and we can talk. I mean you already work for my father. Money is never a problem."

He tightened his grip. I wanted to scream. Letting him win and keep me under his thumb or in jail is not what I wanted for myself.

"Hector, you and I will never be together. I love my boyfriend."

A frown framed his face and I snatched my hand away. "Fuck your boyfriend. Things can change, Charlie."

"What are you saying?"

"Think about the promotion." He gleamed. He reached for the papers and left the office.

"Prick," I mumbled behind his back.

I strolled out of the room and back to my office where I shut and locked my door. Picking up the phone, I dialed, waiting for Nicco to answer.

"Charlie, is everything okay?" Nicco hurriedly answered.

"Promised to call you if I spoke with Hector and I just left a meeting."

Nicco paused. "How did he act?"

"Fine, like nothing even happened last night."

"He's getting bolder."

"Well bold is his middle name because Izan was there in the meeting and they offered me the CEO position."

"You're kidding."

"No, I wish I was. The minute I say yes, I can kiss my

life goodbye."

"They're laying it on thick to have you as the fall guy."

I groaned and sat back in my chair. "I never should have listened to my gut and researched those accounts."

"None of this is your fault."

"Feels like my life is about to fall apart."

A smile in his voice pierced through the phone. "I want you to let me handle your stress."

"Easy to say, Hector and his father are not playing fair."

"Text me later. I know you have the lunch date with the girls," Nicco said.

"Why are you being so calm?"

"You being safe is what keeps me calm."

"Thank you, Nicco."

"You're welcome. Call me when you're ready to get off work. I have the guys outside of the building watching."

Turning toward the window, I pulled the blinds back. I spotted the car a block up the street. "See you later." Smiling, I let him disconnect first and I started to put the phone down when I heard a clicking sound through the line.

I shook off the feeling, tapping my finger against the desk in thought. I jumped up and walked out, looking around at everyone. I might have been paranoid, but if I was being spied on, I wanted to know who.

"Are you alright, Charlie?" my assistant questioned.

"Fine." I speed walked to Hector's office. The door was wide open, and Elaine was sitting on the edge of the desk. I looked away and pretended to go into the supply room.

"Calm down, Charlie. He won't hurt you," I repeated

to myself.

The knob twisted. I rushed to grab something when Craig pushed it open. "Hey, Charlie."

I waved a stack of paper in my hand. "Ran out of paper for my printer." I strolled out of the room and to my office, passing Hector's closed door.

* * *

I noticed Amelia cheeks reddened when talking about her husband from the first moment his name was brought up. Amelia was funny and Cyrah surprisingly showed a softer side of herself and not what the tabloids always reported. Knowing I was sitting with a real celebrity actress and she's down to earth made it even more special. Molly had to work but arranged for our lunch date to be in a private room at the restaurant they frequented together. The restaurant wasn't too crowded.

"Charlie, I have to tell you. Nicco is so infatuated with you," Cyrah teased.

My cheeks rose high automatically at the mention of Nicco. Over time our conversations had gotten deeper, and he was sweet and charming. At the same time, I felt safe and protected.

"I like him."

"So, pretending to be dating has worked out for you two," Amelia giggled.

"How did you two meet your husbands?"

"Amelia, you go first." Cyrah lifted her glass of wine.

"Surprised Nicco never said how Aydin saved my life."

"I know the basic stuff, but how did you fall in love?"

"I worked for him and he hated me." Amelia shrugged

and three of us laughed.

"Seriously."

Amelia nodded. "I was his assistant and the man was so grumpy, but I broke down his walls and we've been married ever since."

"And Nasir and I hated each other, but when I needed protection, he took on the position and we started dating," Cyrah explained.

"Wow."

Amelia poured more wine for me. "Now you and Nicco are becoming close."

"The other night was scary, and I thought I lost him."

Cyrah spooned up more of her dessert. "Their jobs are dangerous, but over time it becomes second nature to not worry."

I blushed. "He asked me out a real date."

Amelia high-fived me. "Good."

"Let him treat you to dinner and show you the real him," Cyrah instigated.

"Is it bad I have strong feelings already and we've barely kissed?"

"Love has no timeline," Amelia remarked.

"On top of a date, I asked him to escort me to a work function and my boss will be there."

"Hector, right?" Amelia challenged.

"Yes, and he's tried for so long to get me to fall for him, but I feel like he might do something to Nicco if I reject him."

Cyrah raised her right brow. "Does Nicco know?"

"Yes. Hector kind of got aggressive."

"How so?" Amelia frowned.

"Felt like if I turned down the promotion and him, I might lose someone close to me."

Amelia and Cyrah stared at each other. "What?"

Cyrah sat back in her seat. "Tell Nicco."

"What if I'm wrong and I misunderstood him?"

Amelia shook her head. "Your gut is never wrong. Hector is bad news."

"I have to tell Nicco for sure."

"What about your family?" Cyrah investigated.

"They've called wanting me to come and bring Nicco. I'm scared to get them involved, especially with Hector roaming around."

"Only way to keep them safe is to inform everyone what's happening," Cyrah replied.

"True. The more people are aware, the better to catch Hector and his father," Amelia agreed.

"How are the kids?" I changed the subject, ready to rid my life of Hector and his father.

"Great and spoiled by their father," Amelia groaned.

"Happy you two came out. I know you both are really busy and have lives."

"We know what this life is like being married to a SEAL, never having to worry about being alone." Amelia grabbed my hand.

"Well Nicco and I are fake dating to trick Hector."

"Not for long," Cyrah tittered.

"He's a great guy."

Amelia cut into her food. "Where is he taking you on the date?"

"I have no clue."

"You should find a really cute dress that shows off those curves, honey." Cyrah snapped her fingers.

"My last date was probably six or more months ago."

Amelia cleared her throat. "Time to get back in the ring and see what can happen."

"It might change things between Nicco and I."

"That's a good thing, right?" Amelia hinted.

"Yes and no."

"Stop self-sabotaging your thoughts."

"Nicco is great and I like him, but what will we do after Hector is arrested?"

"You are scared he really isn't into you other than keeping you safe?" Cyrah's quizzed.

I know the doubt is weird, but some men got off on saving women and moving on to the next thing on their list to build their egos.

"Any man would be honored to date you and marry you, Charlie. Personally, I think Nicco is smitten with you as much as you are with him. Put those doubts away and enjoy dinner," Amelia said.

"Thanks."

"I am full. How about we get the guards to take us to the mall to find something for you to wear tonight?" Cyrah demanded.

"Shopping sounds nice." Amelia reached in her purse and pulled out her card to pay.

"Shopping it is!" Cyrah clapped her hands, finished off her wine, and we laughed some more while leaving the restaurant.

"Guess Nicco spared no expense with protection." I stared at the four SUV's sitting at the curb.

"He's just like Aydin and Nasir. An alpha male who will die before they let anyone hurt their woman." Amelia scooted over, getting in the car.

"Nasir always trips out on me. *Woman, you lost your mind if you think you're driving*." Cyrah dropped her voice low, impersonating her husband.

Laughing at their jokes, the car moved into traffic and

Amelia showed off pictures of her kids. Cyrah talked about her next movie role coming up and asked if we wanted to come to the premiere party.

Lifting my ringing phone to see Hector's name made me suspicious and had me looking behind me to see if he followed me.

Scanning around, nothing stood out. "Hello."

Hector spoke. "Charlie, glad you picked up."

"What can I do for you, Hector?"

Amelia and Cyrah got quiet.

"I'm sending you the details of the dinner layout and your car pickup will arrive at eight p.m.," Hector explained.

I was definitely turning down his suggestion. "A car won't be necessary, Hector."

"As the new CEO, we must insist you take the perks of a driver," he pushed.

"I have not given you an answer."

He went silent.

I pulled the phone from my ear. "Hello?"

Hector growled. "Charlie, my father is counting on you and me working alongside you."

I rushed to get him off the phone. "Right now is not a good time."

"Where are you?"

Hot tears started to well in my eyes. "Out."

"With him?"

I grimaced at him constantly pushing my buttons. "Hector, that's none of your business."

"Think about what I said. Your life would be better with me." Hector disconnected the call. Knowing Nicco would have a fit if he knew Hector was adamant we arrive in his car, I needed to put a stop to his antics and soon.

Chapter 9

Nicco

Locking our hands together, I helped her to sit in the chair and came around to the other side of the table and sat down. Once work finished up, I came home to nap, shower, and get ready for our date. Picking up flowers became the first order of business, even though I didn't know her favorite. I wanted to make a good impression and it worked. The roses hadn't left her hands all night.

"You look handsome."

I raked my eyes over her face. "Are you going to tell me what happened on the call?"

Charlie seemed off tonight. "How do you know about a call?"

"Amelia told me."

She leaned forward and put her elbows on the table, muttering, "I forgot."

"When you were trying on dresses, she called me."

Grinning, she reached to cup my hand. "First date."

"Changing the subject won't make me forget he tried to scare you today."

Giving Hector what he wanted with a fight over Charlie was something I could do and forget my oath to my team. "I know." Charlie looked away.

"So, for now, I will ignore it and enjoy you in this dress and the glow on your face." As soon as I hugged her and took in her sweet perfume, I had to fight to keep it professional and get through dinner without making a move on her. Her legs in those heels made her taller than she normally was and she came up right under my chin.

"Amelia did my makeup and Dedra on the hair."

"Dressed up or down, you are beautiful, Charlie."

Her shyness came out, and she covered her face. "Thank you,"

"Hello, can I get you two started with drinks?"

"A water for me and Charlie?"

"I had wine earlier, just water for now."

The waitress took down our orders and responded, "Coming right up."

"Water?"

"I want to be clear headed for tonight."

"What did you have in mind?"

"Who knows?" Charlie giggled.

"Now tell me about Charlie and what interests her."

"Traveling and work, really. I love the concept of design. Growing up I sketched from the time I was five until I figured out I could get paid to draw."

"Has to be more than work."

The waitress returned with our water. "Have you decided on what you'd like to order?"

"If you don't mind me ordering for you, I come here a lot," I said.

"No, please."

"My background is Mexican and Portuguese. I grew up eating all kinds of flavors."

Charlie gleamed and let me take the lead on ordering. "Can we have an order of Cataplana de Marisco?"

"What did you get us?"

"A mixture of octopus, potatoes, and seafood stew."

"Are you trying to get me to fall asleep before dessert?" she joked.

"Might sound like a lot, but you don't have to eat it all."

"Tell me about your family?"

"Grew up with my parents and a younger brother."

"Are you close?"

"If you saw me, then you saw him all the time. Our mother is the one who taught us to cook and Dad pushed us to always protect our mom and the women in our family."

"That's where you get it from."

"Get what from?"

"Protectiveness, wanting to keep me safe."

I reached my hand out to cover her palm. "For the most part, my job in general I take serious."

Her relaxed nature and beautiful smile poured through tonight. When I got Amelia on the phone earlier and Hector made more underhanded threats, I knew it was time to make him a thing of the past.

"What type of guys do you like?"

"Honestly, the respectful guy, nice, comfortable with himself and me. Understands my dreams and doesn't hide from being with a confident woman. At the same time a little romantic, takes charge and likes to be goofy and loves to travel." Charlie sat back as our food came to the table.

Taking the fork and filling up our plates, we continued talking. "My dating life is my work."

"Are you saying you haven't been with a woman since me?"

There was no reason to lie. All my days have been spent on work or spending time with my family. "Yes."

"That's hard to believe."

Gulping down my water, the waitress refilled our cups. "True though. No girlfriend in the last year or two."

"Nicco...oh my god, the food is delicious." Charlie moaned, putting more food in her mouth.

"Keep moaning and something else will go in your mouth." I smirked.

She coughed at my announcement, and I pushed her water toward her.

"You make me nervous."

Considering what she said earlier of not having a relationship in a long while, it made me think to take things slow. "I hope in a good way."

"Very good."

My fingers slid up her arm. "After dinner, then dessert." I winked at her.

"I like you, Nicco. A lot."

I put my fork down and focused my attention on Charlie. "But."

"No, I like you more and more as we've gotten closer even under these false pretenses of a fake relationship. My only concern is what happens afterwards."

"Afterwards?"

"You catch Hector and he gets locked up. Are you moving on? Was all this work just to use me and then leave?"

Not liking where her mind was going, I scooted back,

stood up, and reached for her hand. "What are you doing?"

"I want you to listen to me well."

Glancing around the room, her eyes widened in embarrassment. "We're in the middle of a restaurant."

"So?"

"Nicco, people are staring." Charlie glanced around.

"That means you're the most stunning woman they've ever seen." Charlie stretched her arms around my neck. "Meeting you was a fluke. The moment I laid eyes on you I knew I wanted you."

"For more than business purposes?"

"Way more." Rubbing a hand up and down her back, Charlie pushed up on her toes to kiss me."

"Take me home."

"Are you done eating?"

"I'm ready for dessert."

* * *

She gasped as her body erupted in chills. There was something so tender about her actions, stroking the back of my head. The scent of her arousal drove me crazy. Anticipation for more launched through her body as she squeezed the back of my head. Need slammed into my chest. I was ready to feel her pussy. I kissed a blazing trail up her thigh and nipped at her shoulder. I pushed her right leg wider and pressed my stiff dick against her core, ready to drive home.

"Nicco," she whimpered, cupping the back of my head, capturing my lips.

I slid my fingers through her hair, stroking slowly in and out, and groaned at her warmth.

"Charlie, I know it's too early, but you're stuck with me."

She nodded, wrapping both hands around my waist, and pulled me in closer. "Ughhh, yes..." she gasped.

The sight of her pleasure encompassed her face. "Fuck me harder," she begged. She pressed her breasts against my chest. I bent down and placed a kiss on her soft lips. I swirled my tongue around and sucked on her bottom lip. Grasping her left breasts, squeezing, pulling back suck on her nipples and moving my hips.

"Yesss..."

Wanting another taste, I moved below and strummed my fingers in her pussy, spreading her legs wider.

I smirked as she arched her back off the bed and listened to her fall into an orgasmic bliss. If we were going to be together forever, I needed to take care of Hector before he came after her again.

"Uhmmm, oh...shit," Charlie moaned.

As I massaged the bottom of her feet, I lightly gripped her ankle and pressed both legs back further to get deeper, feeling her juices flow down on top of the sheets. Slowly removing myself, I gazed down at her suctioning me back in, causing me to pump faster and faster.

"Yeah, Charlie, give it to me."

"Nicco, please..." she pleaded.

Charlie unraveled beneath me. Clasped our hands together, pushed above her head, I drove my length back and forth. I groaned, teasing her lips, and I dropped my head down, about ready to burst.

"I'm about to come...."

Burying myself to the hilt, I slowly tongued her swollen nipple, losing my mind at the sensations, the sparks we'd made together. Against all logic she melted against me and I instantly got harder.

"Come for me baby."

I gently spanked my hand down and tweaked her nipple.

"Fucking beautiful, Charlie."

"Nicco." Charlie moaned, turning me onto my back and rolling her hips. My breath caught at the tightness of her body welcoming me and sparked a protectiveness inside me. *She's mine.*

One hand entwined in her hair, and I smacked her on the ass with the other. She rocked back and forth. Wanting her closer, I wrapped both hands around her, burying my nose in her neck, smelling her sweet scent.

"Charlie, you're dangerous for me."

She pulled back. "You're dangerous for me."

We both grinned. She flicked her tongue across my bottom lip, clinging tight, and writhed against my erection as I came inside of her.

* * *

Days later, standing at the counter with my hands wrapped around her waist, I listened to her closely tell me she wanted me to meet her parents today and that she wanted to update them on her getting a promotion to CEO of Torrio business. I flatly told her that she's not taking the job. Hector was setting up everything to hand her over to the DEA as soon as she agreed to the position.

I cut the onions and peppers, then tossed them into the pan for scrambled eggs.

"I plan on turning him down at dinner. He thinks he can intimidate me and I'd just go along with him."

Standing back against the counter, I watched her pull plates out of the cabinet. Being around her made my days better. Watching her become familiar with my home brought a smile to my face.

"Hector has one more time to try and get in your face."

"He knows we're together and is still trying to force my hand."

Holding her palm, I kissed the back of her hand. "My hand will be forced to go across his face if he steps to you one more time."

"I might quit working there."

Since our first night of love making, I have wanted her more and more. "Is that what you want?"

"I can find a job somewhere else doing what I love."

"What about opening your own business?"

Taking both of our plates, I followed her to the table, while she carried the orange juice. "I do have some savings but opening a business can be hard without backing."

"Give yourself credit, Charlie. You're smart, funny, and charming. Any bank will fight to give you a loan."

"Thank you, Nicco."

Listening to her talk on the phone with her parents, I heard them talking and encouraging her. "How are they?"

Charlie brushed a soft hand down my chest. "Good. How do you feel about us going? I mean, it's kind of fake."

"Fine."

Staring at me she smirked. "So you and me having sex again."

"Not after another night of you screaming my name."

She shrugged her shoulders. "You were incredible. I give you props."

"Watching you go from shy to sexy kitten on my dick surprised me."

Covering her face with her hands, she giggled. "I might be a little shy, but I know how to ride a dick, sir."

I choked on my juice. "Charlie."

She laughed. "What?" She poured syrup on her pancakes.

"Talking about riding my dick is going to cause problems."

"Problems for who?" She winked, and I shook my head.

"Dangerous woman."

"Are you off today?"

"I am. The boys are following up on a lead and I decided to take the day off since you have the weekend off."

"How many hours do you work on average?"

I exhaled a breath. "At least sixty or more a week."

"Jesus."

"TN Security Company handles all sorts of clients from political figures, celebrities, and mobsters, to regular joes."

I pulled my toast apart and threw it in my mouth.

She watched me. "Today we should do something you like."

"Have you rock climbed?"

"No, is it hard?"

"I like doing more endurance type of stuff; biking, rock climbing, basketball, any type of sport."

"Great. I have a boyfriend that wants me to keep my hair sweated out." She rolled her eyes and I laughed.

"Boyfriend," I teased.

"The things you did should only come from my

boyfriend," she cackled. I leaned forward, kissing her on the cheek, then moved over to her lips and deepened the kiss, pushing my tongue in her mouth.

An hour later we got dressed and I brought her to the indoor rock-climbing center I like to visit with my brother and the guys at work. Charlie looked nervous in her gear and I assured her we'd take it slow. After a while she got the hang of everything. Making it to the top, I saw the glee in her eyes.

"That was fun!" Charlie cheered.

"First time for a beginner."

She poked her lip out. "For a beginner, I still got the hang of things."

"Baby, the amount of times you almost dropped, I had to help you back."

A teasing smile spread over her face. "Are you saying maybe I should stick to something else?"

I bit my lip. "If I said yes, would you be mad?"

"No, I will just go another turn."

"Aren't your parents expecting us?" A flush stung my cheeks.

She turned her face away and looked down. "Nice try."

I held up both hands. "I'll follow your lead."

"First one to the bottom has to buy the other dinner."

"Go!" I shouted.

Her eyes widened as I lowered myself to the ground.

"You cheated!" she fussed, climbing down slowly, and I laughed. After getting us out of the gear and buying us a bottle of water, I ushered her out of the building. I spotted the team parked in the lot waiting for me to leave. As we left the facility, I answered my phone.

"Bro, where are you at?" Emmanuel's voice blasted

through the speaker.

"Out with Charlie," I told him, catching my breath.

Emmanuel's gravelly voice queried, "Who's Charlie?"

"My girl."

"Miss Big Boobs," Emmanuel taunted. Ready to ignore him, I started to hang up.

Charlie tittered and I took the phone off speaker. "Call her Charlie, asshole."

"She's hot with titties."

"Mommy should have left you at the hospital."

Listening to him laugh with his friends in the background, I focused on the light ahead.

Charlie held a hand to her mouth and laughed at him.

"I apologize for my crazy brother."

"He's fine."

"Does she have a sister?"

"Why are you calling me?"

"Hanging with my boys and wanting to see if you had time to play the game."

"Charlie invited me to meet her parents."

"She pregnant?"

Ignoring his question, I hung the phone up. I threw it in the cupboard and pressed the gas while it rang again.

"Why are you ignoring your brother?"

"He's an idiot," I grumbled.

"I like the carefree Nicco," Charlie told me. She lifted her hand to caress the back of my neck as I drove.

Arriving a short while later, I parked out front of her parents' house in Chickasaw Gardens. A woman who I assumed was her mother stood at the front door at the top of the stairs. Charlie took my hand and sauntered up the walkway. She released my hand to hug her mother, then she introduced me.

"Mom, this is Nicco."

"Nice to meet you, Nicco."

"Nice to meet you, ma'am." I wrapped my hand around Charlie's waist.

"Come inside. Your dad's almost finished with the lobster." Her mom held the door, and we headed in. I looked around to see pictures of Charlie and her siblings hanging on the wall. The house was a large brick home, which felt warm and inviting, with a fireplace, and a large TV hung on the wall.

"Hi honey." Her dad appeared with both arms open.

"Dad!"

"Let me look at you," he said.

"I thought you told me you'd work on your diet?" Charlie pouted, rubbing his belly.

"Girl, leave me alone." He pushed her hand away and she laughed.

"Charlie, it's a lost cause trying to get the man to eat a vegetable." Her mom rolled her eyes.

"The family wants you here forever. You know your cholesterol is high," Charlie fussed.

"Who are you?' Her dad pointed at me.

I extended my hand for him to shake. "Hello, sir. I'm Nicco."

"Nicco, what are you doing with my daughter?"

Parents have never been an issue for me because most of the women I dated never lasted long and ended after a few months. Sitting with her parents, I knew she meant something to me and I wanted to make a great impression. Answering his questions might put Charlie off, but I had to be honest about my feelings. To me, time didn't matter when it came to the person you knew belonged to you.

Chapter 10

Charlie

My parents never really got on my case about a guy I dated unless they saw me being mistreated, so seeing my Dad and Nicco already laughing and joking early on felt good. He pressed a kiss to the back of my hand. I passed the bowl of mac and cheese to him and took a bite of the lobster.

"Nicco, our daughter tells us you work in security."

"Yes, sir. Being an ex-SEAL, I work with my brothers that started the company."

"Do you have any kids?" Dad started his twenty-one questions.

"No."

"Do you want kids in the future?" Mom challenged him.

"Can we date first before you start talking about grandkids?" I asked. I smacked my forehead and rolled my eyes.

My parents laughed and Nicco joined in with them.

"Stop encouraging their craziness. Same way you have a crazy brother, these two are top notch."

"Charlie's one of our babies. She means everything to us, so just know if you hurt my child, I have no problem getting the gun." Dad grunted, and Nicco smirked.

"I understand. My plans are we continue getting to know each other."

"Glad to hear. Charlie, is everything good at your job?" Mom quipped.

Capturing Nicco's stare, I gulped down the lobster and wiped my hands clean on the napkin.

"At first I wanted to keep you in the dark, but some things at work are getting out of hand."

"How out of hand?" Mom grabbed my dad's hand.

"Someone may be trying to frame me."

"Her boss is framing her for embezzlement."

"Nicco." I was trying to keep some of the details from them.

Dad waved his hand at me. "Let him talk, Charlie. Go on, Nicco."

I prayed this wouldn't stress my parents too much. I threw my head back and closed my eyes briefly, waiting for the big reveal.

Nicco caressed my thigh under the table. "My team is running point on security for Charlie because she has evidence on her boss."

"Charlie, I knew something was fishy with that company. I have half a mind to go up there with my gun," Dad argued.

"Honey, calm down." Mom patted his arm.

"She's not going back there," Dad insisted.

"Dad, please relax. I know what I'm doing."

"You're putting yourself in danger!" Dad shouted.

"Charlie's right. If she quit right now, it would look

suspicious. I promise your daughter is safe with me." Nicco being here gave me comfort. The problem was my parents would go into protective mode and want me to live with them until Hector's locked up.

"How much evidence do you need to get these guys?" Mom quizzed.

"It's complicated. Hector's family is locked into so much corruption and the Mafia."

Mom held a hand to her chest, and her mouth dropped open in shock. "Mafia? Oh, Jesus."

My thoughts were all over the place. Taking the plunge and informing my parents probably put me in the worst position.

"How safe are we?" Mom asked.

"I can have some men stationed with you." Nicco reached into his pocket, pulling out a cell phone.

"That won't be necessary," Dad replied.

"Listen to the man. Whatever Charlie is dealing with is serious and I want all of us covered," Mom shared. She stood, walked around the table, and bent down to give me a hug.

I pushed my plate back. My appetite was gone completely and my mind drained from talking about Hector and his family. I still needed to give him an answer about the promotion, and he'd insisted I do it at the dinner. But I wanted to step out and show him that I couldn't be intimidated.

"Where are you going?" Nicco asked.

"To the restroom."

Giving him a soft smile, I went into the bathroom upstairs. I shut the door behind me and dialed Hector's number.

"Hello."

A giggling voice spoke on the phone. "Yes."

"May I speak with Hector?"

She giggled. "Hector's busy at the moment."

"What the fuck are you doing with my phone?" Hector shouted. I heard shuffling and the dial tone.

"That was strange," I whispered. I shook off my thoughts and washed my hands to go back downstairs.

Nicco stood with a bag in his hands. "Your mom gave us some leftovers."

"She likes you." I reached my arms around his waist, resting my head on his chest.

"I like them, too."

"Charlie, keep us updated now. We know you won't move in here, so the easiest thing to do is call every day," Dad demanded.

"Okay, Dad."

Mom kissed me on the cheek, and Dad pecked my forehead. After yawning and stretching we decided to head out for the evening and head back to his place for the night.

* * *

Laughter echoed in the hall. Craig and a few of the guys talked about starting up a sports league for the office. After the weekend, I came into work bright and early, ready to tackle more information on Hector and his father. My plan of attack while everyone was working off site came perfectly timed. Pushing the door of the basement open I slipped in, turning the light on and running to the filing cabinets to start researching. Hector talked about Videl. The last few accounts needed to be looked at and I offered.

"A-F," I muttered, flicking through each folder. Typing out the report on Videl's workload I got the top five and worked my way backwards.

"Charlie."

I froze in place. "Hector." The basement was usually quiet. No one, especially Hector, would ever come down here.

"What are you doing?"

"I thought you had a meeting out of town." I shut the drawer, putting the files behind my back.

"It was canceled." Hector shut and locked the door. He stalked over, placing an index finger under my chin.

"Answer my question."

"What question?"

He smirked. "What are you doing in the basement?"

"You asked me to look into some of Videl's workload, remember? Clients wanted an update on how things will run with him gone."

Hector shoved his hands in his pockets. "I thought I told you I would handle everything dealing with Videl."

"Well, my goal is to lighten your load. Let me get back upstairs." I went to slide around him, but he stuck his hand out to block me.

"You look beautiful today."

"Thanks."

"Have you given some thought to my question?"

"I have, and I won't take the position."

"Charlie, you're a hard case to crack." Hector popped his knuckles, backing me up against the cabinet.

"What are you doing, Hector?"

"Trying to understand you."

"Nothing to understand. I work for your father."

He propped both hands above my head. "Tell me what you really want and I can make it happen."

He reached to touch my hair, and I stepped back. "I want to do my job and that's all."

"Most women would fall at my feet."

I felt my lunch rise to the top of my throat. Throwing up on him would probably get me out of here sooner. "I am not like most women."

"That makes you special."

"Mr. Torrio!" Elaine spat.

Hector groaned and removed his hands. I went to walk off and he grabbed my arm. "We're not done."

"I have to get back to work."

Elaine glared at me as I went up the stairs. I stopped for a brief moment to hear arguing between the two.

"Are you sleeping with her?" Elaine yelled.

"Watch your mouth, bitch," Hector growled.

A loud smack sliced the air and I jogged faster back to my office. I quickly shut the door then leaned up against it as I tried to calm my breathing.

"He's crazy."

Going through the files, the same numbers populated and my signature was documented as the final sign off for the last three deals.

I removed my glasses and rubbed my eyes. Hector had everything running in his favor. No matter how much he pretended to like me, all he wanted was for me to take the fall.

Me: *I need to talk to you.*

Nicco: *Should I come up there?*

Me: *No, but Hector tried to make a pass at me.*

Nicco: *On my way.*
Me: *Wait! He's gone, I promise.*
Nicco: *Still, driving to you now.*
Me: *I was able to get some documents from the basement.*
Nicco: *Anything good?*
Me: *I think so.*
Nicco: *What about the pen?*
Me: *Oh crap, I left it in his office.*
Nicco: *No need to go back to his office.*
Me: *He's out for lunch, give me a second.*

I closed out of our thread and jumped up, sprinting to Hector's office, seeing the door open and his assistant gone. I rushed in and shut it behind me and the blinds were already closed. I searched through his desk drawers for the pen.

"Hector knows you're here?"

"Craig."

"What are you doing, Charlie?" Craig quipped.

I grabbed the first file I saw. "Hector wanted me to pick up a new account." Walking around the desk I noticed the pen on the edge of the coffee table.

"Craig, did you get a chance to talk with him about the sports teams?"

Craig nodded. "Actually, he said I could lead the match up."

Smiling, I reached for the pen and started toward the door. "That's great. I left my pen. See you later."

"Yeah, see you later," Craig answered.

Back in my office I picked up my phone seeing Nicco's responses.

Nicco: *Charlie, wait!*
Nicco: *Charlie, answer the phone.*

Nicco: *Where are you?*
Nicco: *I'm outside.*
"Shit, he's angry."

Picking up my purse, jacket, and briefcase, I put all of the evidence I'd gathered in the case and closed it. Leaving, I waved goodbye to my assistant.

I glanced over my shoulder and no one paid any attention to me leaving in a hurry. I kept my head down until I made it to Nicco's truck and hopped inside.

"Did he touch you?" Nicco turned my face left to right, cupping my chin.

"No, I promise." I fastened my seatbelt and passed the pen to him, clasping my hands in my lap.

"I'm going to take you home and we can go over what you pulled."

"Will Wesley be able to check the recording?"

"He should. Downloading might take a few hours."

"I'm starving."

Passing by the cars, Nicco left a hand on my leg. I stared out of the window until we made it to his apartment.

"I had groceries already delivered and put away. Go inside and shower so I can start an early dinner."

"That sounds good."

"Charlie." Nicco pulled me into his chest, gently rubbing a finger across my bottom lip.

"Yes."

"The minute he put you in an uncomfortable position, I wanted to kill him."

"He can't hurt me."

"My goal is to make sure of that. Go take a shower."

Sliding his tongue over my lip, I groaned into his touch, pressing my hands to the back of his head.

He pulled back. "Go before I have you on the couch."

"I wouldn't mind."

"After we eat."

Remembering him having my legs pinned to my chest as he sucked on my clit sent chills down my spine.

Chapter 11

Nicco

The sight of her bare, soft body had me unbearably hard. I gripped her ass and placed a kiss on her lips. I watched her lie on the couch with her legs spread wide. I ripped off my shirt and pants. My fingers curled around her hand, kissing the back of her knuckles.

"Make me yours." Charlie inched upward, then carefully circled her hands around the back of my neck. I took her leg, folding it around my waist, and pushed forward.

"Mmmmmm...." she purred.

"Just breathe, baby."

Her breath hitched. Her back arched. With feathered kisses, I took her mouth with unrelenting passion.

Taking my other hand, I teased her clit. Charlie rode my hand as I thrusted forward. I wanted to feel her from the back, so I slipped out and helped her to get on all fours. I was clutching her waist, stroking her faster and faster.

Her body molded to my touch.

Her scent filled my lungs like a last breath.

Meeting her woke up something, woke up a part of me I'd kept locked away and now that she had opened that door, I needed her in my life forever.

If anyone fucked with her, they'd have to answer to me.

Looking over her shoulder, she bit her lip, showing off a sexy smirk.

Smacking her ass again, she moaned.

"Keep looking at me like that and you'll find yourself not able to walk tomorrow," I taunted, leaning over her back, whispering in her ear.

Dragging kisses down her back, I locked our fingers together above her head. I pumped forward, feeling sweat fall on our slick bodies. My breathing was heightened, and I groaned in her ear at our slick warmth.

"You can take it, baby. Feel how deep I can get."

She nodded, shattering into a million glowing pieces, sweat glistening her smooth, warmth skin. Imprinting my name all over her body was my goal.

"Let me hear you, baby." I kissed the back of her ear.

Strumming her clit, I felt her wetness drenching her legs.

"Fuck, you're wetting me up, Charlie."

"Arghhhh, Nicco. It's too much." Charlie buried her head in the couch.

"Love, just enough. You're such a good girl. Take this dick."

Pulling her flush against me, I licked the back of her neck. Charlie turned to kiss me, cuffing the side of my chin and I grunted, still rocking into her.

"Sit back and let me ride you, baby." Charlie pushed me up against the couch, in the reverse cowgirl, bouncing her ass on my dick.

Cupping my balls, my head fell back, and I covered my eyes with my arm trying not to come too quickly. Charlie breathed in deep soul-drenching breaths.

"Shit!" I felt like I was drowning in her world and never wanted to escape.

She claimed me as much as I claimed her at this moment. Her cries of deep lust filled the room as our skin slapped. A surge of energy burst through her and she clasped her ankles, bucking on top of me.

"Charlie," I groaned, my body responding as my toes popped and my stomach clenched.

The urge to release was overwhelming.

The sight of her like that set a fire inside of me so hot, I almost hated that she had sex with other men before me.

"You ready to come, Nicco?"

Contentment and peace flowed between us. "Yes, god damn, your pussy."

She giggled. "I'm right there with you."

We both orgasmed at the same time. She fell into my arms with her back to my chest. I held her tight as I released my seed and caught my breath.

Locking up my office, I checked my suit and pocket to make sure I had everything for dinner tonight. Hector made a move and it was time to end the back and forth games and shut him down for good. I looked up at the sound of the whistles and giggles as Molly and Amelia stood around the front desk with Charlie.

"Hey, Nicco, you look sharp," Amelia said.

"Thanks, Amelia, but I doubt your husband would like to hear about his wife lusting after the hottest guy on the team," I teased and felt a sting on the back of my head.

"Watch your mouth," Aydin glared at me.

Amelia tittered next to Charlie, and I frowned. "You're supposed to be on my side," I fussed.

"Ahh, poor baby." Charlie laughed, stretching her arms out to embrace me. She and the girls had gotten close over the past few weeks and I was glad she had other women that understood our work. The hours we spent working could sometimes go more than twenty-four and I didn't want her thinking I was some type of playboy that went out clubbing every weekend. Having fun every few months wasn't bad, but I took my job seriously. Pulling Charlie into my chest, I nuzzled my nose in her neck and pecked her lips.

"Hate that Hector's going to see you look this delicious before I lock his ass up."

Charlie cupped my chin. "Are you sure it will be safe?"

"Positive, unless he makes the wrong move."

"Izan tried talking to me at the office, but we kept getting interrupted."

"Then tonight try and get him to spill some secrets."

"Long as you and the guys are there."

Aydin cocked his head letting us know it was time to leave. Amelia, Charlie, and Cyrah all walked out in front of the guys heading to the limo. Charlie was able to get them tickets at the same table, making it even easier to get close to Izan and his team.

I held the door open, and Charlie got in. I grasped her hand and shut the door. I listened to them talk about their days. Two cars filled with our team trailed behind us for security. Nasir and Aydin in the front car secured the location details on the phone. I watched the sparkle in Charlie's eyes. By becoming friends, even Dedra got to hang out with the other wives of the team.

The limo stopped at the light a few blocks from the venue seconds later pulled up to the entrance. I glanced at the two-story building, wondering how much security Hector had established. We all waited, going through a security check. I took her hand and strolled inside. I pulled her close to my side.

"He's right there." Charlie gestured to Hector laughing with a woman and man near the check in table.

"Keep calm and play it smooth."

"Just nervous." Charlie smiled, shaking hands with a few co-workers, introducing me and the rest of the wives.

Lights dimmed in the banquet hall. Classical jazz filled the space. Izan Torrio, who was surrounded by his guards and his henchman, threw his head back in a laugh. My skin pricked wanting to lock him up where he stood, but I knew the better option was to get more evidence. Charlie mixed and mingled with a few of her staff. Aydin approached me, passing me an earpiece I put it in my ear and took the gun he snuck through security with the wait-staff he paid off.

"Remember, don't make a move until they force our hand," Aydin demanded.

Scanning the room, a few more people started to file in and the announcer directed us to take our seats. The speakers began to start, the fakeness of how the Torrio family was giving back to the community rolled off their tongues and I wanted to shut it completely down. Taking a sip of the water, I clasped a hand on Charlie's thigh.

"Charlie, I was looking for you," Hector said.

Hector stood with another man hovering over our

table. Charlie glanced up. "Sorry I wanted to get to our table," Charlie explained.

"I'd love to introduce you to a few important people."

Charlie looked from me to Hector. "Umm sure. Do you mind, Nicco?"

"I'm sure he's fine with you leaving him for a few minutes. I mean, he understands you're a working woman, right?" Hector challenged.

I gritted my teeth, wanting to slam my fist into his face. "As long as you promise to give me a kiss first," I taunted Hector.

Charlie smiled and moved in closer, pecked me on my cheek, and then on the lips. Standing, she walked off with Hector, and his hand went around her back before I could snatch it down. Charlie backed away, putting distance between them.

"I take it he's the one you're trying to take down?" Cyrah wondered.

"Him and his father at the front table." I gestured to the head table where Izan sat with his family. I gulped the rest of my water, as the staff came around placing food on the table, and started to eat.

"We're going to move around the room." Aydin motioned toward me. I stood with him looking to the area Charlie walked over to and saw she wasn't standing there.

"You see Charlie?" I muttered, moving through the crowd. Aydin and Nasir followed me.

"Wasn't she just talking to some guy with Hector?" Nasir responded. I shook my head, moving at the speed of light, and I bum rushed through a crowd of people.

"Hey, what's your problem?" a man argued, spilling some of his drink on himself.

"Where's Charlie?" I gripped the suit jacket of the guy I saw walking off with Hector and Charlie.

"Excuse me?"

"Where is Charlie? She was just talking with you?"

"I have no clue who you're talking about."

"Motherfucker, she is my woman!" I shouted, balling up my fist.

"Nicco, Hector's not here," Nasir whispered. The hair on the back of my neck rose.

He grinned. "I suggest you take your hands off me, if you want to see her again," the guy said.

I raised my hand and slugged him in the face. "What the fuck!" A few screams and shouts were heard.

"Security! I want him arrested," he growled.

"They got her!" I shoved him, reaching to grab my gun.

"Nicco, not here!" Aydin commanded, and I knew I should listen to him, but if this was Amelia and the time she was in trouble, he'd turn the place inside out.

"Nothing you do will work. I think it's best you leave." Izan stood in front of us.

"Where's Hector?"

"My son and I will file a lawsuit for the harassment you've thrown toward me and my family." Izan helped the man off the floor.

"Pray your son doesn't end up dead."

"Nicco! Let's go!" Nasir shouted. I sprinted out of the main banquet, helping the rest of the ladies get to the car. Scanning the building, I watched security on high alert, watching us and talking in a crowd.

"He's got her."

"Wesley was able to get a picture of her leaving in a car with Hector."

"Where?"

"Before I show you, I need you to stay calm."

"I'm calm."

Aydin eyed me and then nodded for Nasir to pass the phone toward me. Seeing Charlie in his arms, passed out, made my stomach drop.

"I'm going to kill him."

"We're going to kill him."

"Police are on their way," Amelia said.

"Fucking paid off. Probably will be invited to sit and eat," I growled.

"What direction did the car go?"

"Two vans came out and split off. Hard to tell, it was underground through the scope," Aydin detailed.

"We need to split up," I suggested.

"Take Nasir with you. Keep your phone on at all times. If we get word, trace our location," Aydin expressed, and I started to remove my suit jacket and dressed in my vest and equipment.

"Bring our girl back, Nicco," Amelia told me.

Holding the picture of Charlie knocked out, his filthy hands around her body pissed me off. I promised her that I would protect her from Hector. We rolled up to the Torrio office building twenty minutes later. I shoved the door wide open and was stepping out when a hand latched down to stop me.

"Going in like Rambo won't help Charlie," Nasir argued.

"Nasir, if she's in there, I'm going in with or with you."

Nasir exclaimed, "We're all going in together, but the right way."

Aydin nodded in agreement. "Nasir's right, trying to bombard Hector will only get her hurt and us killed."

"Dealing with the mob is the one time you really need to think clearly, Nicco."

"Not the war, but a battle we need to win," I said.

"Charlie is safe. Hector wants her alive because he needs her," Nasir mentioned.

"Keep telling yourself he wouldn't do anything stupid after listening to the recording and matching it up with her secretary. I have no faith they'll play nice."

"Crazy. All along, her biggest opposition is her assistant working against her," Wesley remarked, and I agreed with a nod.

Reaching for another gun to put in my sock, I slammed the door shut staring up at the building ready to burn it down.

"How sure are we that he's here?" Nasir questioned.

"Only two places I can think of him taking her—here or his home."

"The other guys are moving into his place now. Maybe we should wait for the call," Wesley suggested.

"No," I growled, stalking up the walkway to the building.

"Shit!" Nasir spat.

Chapter 12

Charlie

"She's going to be a problem, Hector."

"Let me run my business."

"What about me and you?"

"Shut up and go check on the things and make sure no one comes in here."

The door slammed, my breathing spiked, and sweat trickled down my chest. I regretted not quitting the first chance I had when I noticed everything happening around me. Loud footsteps pricked at my ears. The door opened, and the light flicked on like last time. At that moment, I finally noticed the dirt and rust in the room from not coming down here in so long. He stood back, staring me down, and I wanted to say something. The tape on my mouth prevented me from screaming and my wrists were tied to the chair. A flicker of anger crossed his face. He came closer, sucking his teeth.

"One scream and you're dead."

I nodded, not ready for my life to end. He slowly removed the tape from my mouth. Tears trailed down my cheeks, and he wiped each one away. But they kept coming. Slowly his finger moved down my cheek and my neckline. I tried to squirm to get him to move away.

"You look beautiful tonight, Charlie."

Nothing seemed to matter to him but taking me from Nicco. All his lies would come out. As long as he had me that was his true mission and I fell for it again. "Hector, please."

"Shush."

"If you let me go—"

He raised his hand to cut me off. "Charlie, you never listen to me."

"I...I..." I stuttered, knowing it was pointless to beg, but I would try.

Smirking, he wiped another tear with his finger, then slipped it in his mouth. "It tastes sweet like I knew you would."

"Please, let me go."

"Those breasts are calling my name. I wanted you from the beginning."

"Elaine. What about Elaine?"

"Elaine's nothing to me."

"Did you kill Videl and try to frame me?"

"The truth is, Charlie, you got too close to my business."

Hector's arrogance was the problem and I knew at some point it would cause him to make mistakes.

"My name is on all those accounts. Why, if you like me so much?"

"I do, make no mistake. I've wanted to fuck you for a few years. Also, I needed a reliable person to take the fall for me if we got caught."

"Let me go and we can forget everything."

"Hector, we need to hurry up and go to catch our

flight." Hearing that familiar voice gave me pause. Why would my assistant be here tonight with Hector? They've never had full conversations. I thought she was married with a family.

"You."

Yvonne came into the room smiling. She walked up to Hector and interlocked their hands, trying to kiss him on the lips. He pushed her away.

"Hector!" Yvonne snapped.

Before I could figure out what happened, a shot went off and she fell dead to the ground. Hector placed the gun back in his holster.

"She talks too much."

"She's dead," I whispered.

"I never liked her as your assistant."

No, I wasn't Yvonne's biggest fan after learning she's the one working with Hector but killing her is the last thing I thought he would do. "You killed her!" I cried.

"Only used her to help me get close to you and find out how much you knew."

"I don't understand why you're doing this to me."

"All you had to do was take the job and fall in love with me." Hector caressed my cheek. I tried to back away, but he gripped my chin and pressed a kiss to my lips. I bit his lips and he smacked me across the face.

"Bitch!"

"Help!" I scrambled.

"Keep acting up, Charlie, and I will have to punish you."

The hard look showed an uneasiness between us. "No, I need to get out of here."

"You're not going anywhere, only with me."

"Does your father know?"

"Who do you think made the choice to frame you? My father is the devil in disguise. All the times you thought he praised you."

"What do you want?"

"I will untie you and we will leave to catch our flight. Once we get away, I will work it so your name is not implicated in any business dealings."

"So, you want me to fake being with you?"

"Unlike the fake boyfriend you tried to pawn around here. We are getting married and after a year, I will have the documents destroyed and made untraceable."

"All of this for a fake marriage."

"My father is going to turn everything over to me, and I want you by my side."

"Hector, you can have any woman in the world."

"That's right and I want you."

Hector bent down to kiss me again. All of a sudden, a loud blast at the door knocked it down. The voices running rampant became clear and Nicco stood with a gun in his hand.

Hector yanked me in front of him. "Put the gun down."

Cocking his head to the side, Nicco's eyes scanned me from head to toe.

"Are you hurt? Did he touch you?" Nicco commanded.

"No."

"Shut up! She's mine now. Fuck you," Hector shouted.

"She was never yours. I suggest you let her go and I might spare you."

"Nicco, he's crazy," I mumbled as Hector's hand

wrapped around my mouth. He nudged me back to his chest.

"I got him, Nicco!" Nasir shouted. I didn't know what was happening, but I wanted to get away from Hector as fast as possible.

"We got the evidence. You're going down Hector Torrio."

"What evidence?" Hector grunted.

"A live recording of you." Nicco lifted his cell phone pocket and hit play.

"She's the biggest liability at the moment, but we can control her. Taking care of Videl had to be done. She got too close to the truth," Hector said.

"I expect you to clean up your mess," Izan replied.

"Father, I know in the past I have disappointed you, but she's going to fall at my feet once I blackmail her with these papers."

"If it fails, you kill her and send it to the DEA. My name will not be associated with any bullshit," Izan demanded.

Taking the risk, I bit down hard on his hand. Getting pushed to the side, I crawled away as a shot went off and I stayed down, taking cover behind the side of the wall.

"Clear!" Nasir shouted.

"Charlie! You're safe, baby." Nicco ran to me, lifting me from the ground.

He kissed all over my face, and I hugged him tight.

"Is he dead?" I muttered.

"Him and the secretary," Nicco reminded me.

"My god, he really wanted to kill me."

Feeling his strong arms around me, I felt secure and safe not wanting to let go. Nicco carried me out of the basement and up the stairs to await the ambulance.

"Where are you going?"

"I need to finish debriefing the team, and you need to get to the hospital." Nicco kissed me on the forehead. I grasped his hand.

"No, I want you with me."

"That's going to take a while and I want you checked out."

"Nicco, please. Come with me."

Looking deep into my eyes, he agreed, kissing me and jumping in the back of the ambulance.

"Wesley, let Nasir know to call me. I'm heading to the hospital with Charlie," Nicco announced to his team.

"Glad you're okay, Charlie." Wesley tapped the back of the ambulance, I waved goodbye, listening to them check over my vitals.

* * *

A few weeks later I watched the morning news. The DEA and the local state's attorney were all being arrested along with Izan Torrio for not only money laundering and RICO charges, but murder and conspiracy. The trial was set to start in a few months and they asked if I'd be a witness, but I hadn't made up my mind. Sipping the rest of my coffee, I lounged on the couch thinking of the past events that led me here. Hector wanted to kidnap me and possibly kill me because of some deep twisted love I never led him to believe.

"Morning, beautiful."

"Hey, where are you coming from?"

"Hanging with these idiots." Nicco held the door open for his brother, Nasir, and Wesley to come in with the basketball.

"Charlie, are you still with this clown? I thought we had something special," Emmanuel grinned, holding my hand.

Nicco smacked him on the back of the head. "Touch her and die, bro."

"Nicco, you're whipped," Emmanuel joked.

"Glad to be whipped as long as I have Charlie," Nicco responded, and I giggled.

"How did I get into the conversation?"

Nasir and Wesley burst into laughter. "What are your plans for the day, babe?" Nicco came back with bottles of water for each of the guys and plopped down on the couch next to me.

"I wanted to go by the office and clean out my desk."

Nicco frowned. "No."

Fear showed in his face. "Nicco, I think I will be fine."

"I will go do it."

"I have family pictures and other trinkets I left behind." I felt like a teenager asking my parents for permission.

"Have them ship it to you."

"Hector is no longer there, so I think I will be fine."

"What are they doing about the company anyway with Izan on trial?" Nasir said.

"Izan had the company turned over to Craig of all people and he's the new CEO. I guess he's trying to separate ties from the mafia business."

"He knows what they tried to do to you and he stayed?" Wesley asked.

"Yep, he's always wanted to be top dog."

"Let me shower and then we can drive over there." Nicco stood and walked out of the room.

"Has he told you what he wants for his birthday?" Nasir asked.

"Not really."

"My brother's not a big party guy now, probably family dinner," his brother informed me.

"Him taking care of the case put him in a bigger position with Aydin. More lead cases means him being gone more. Are you ready for that role?" Nasir questioned and I had time to go over in my head and heart whether we'd be together or not. It started as fake. But that led us to becoming best friends and lovers.

"I'm ready."

A few hours later, I met up with my parents after cleaning out my office and tossing the stuff I didn't need any more. I had decided to leave the pictures with my parents. My mom poured us both a glass of hot tea and Nicco stood outside with my dad.

Mom sipped on her drink. "How are you feeling?"

Sighing, I blew over the top. "Better now that he's dead."

"Any more nightmares?"

"No and I took your advice to speak with a therapist."

Mom gently rubbed my hand. "Happy to hear, honey."

"My life could have changed in a split second because of him," I said, snapping my fingers.

"Nicco is a good man. He loves you."

I turned to look out at the backyard from the kitchen. "He asked me to live with him permanently."

"Are you?"

Nodding, I grabbed my tea. "I think I will."

"He's a keeper and takes good care of you, protects you. All your father and I wanted."

"I want you to meet his parents one day."

"Maybe at a wedding." She started her routine of getting me down the aisle.

"Hold your horses, lady."

She poked out her lip. "You both are in your late twenties. It's time to think of your future."

"I want to get back to work in some capacity."

"Take the time to rest for now. It's only been a week since you got back home."

"I hear you, but all my life I worked, drew my designs, and now it feels like starting over."

"Not a bad thing, baby."

I twirled the lemon in my tea. "How is Dad doing?"

"Your father is the same as always—happy in his home. Come on. Let's go out back and see what the men are talking about. Are you two staying for dinner?"

"Yeah, I have to plan his birthday dinner. Can you and Dad come?"

Mom gestured for me to come into the kitchen to help finish prepping. "We'd love to come and meet his family." Life was starting to get back to normal. Soon I could figure out my next steps in my career. Nicco was going to be a big part of my future and I prayed we would work out.

Chapter 13

Nicco

I kissed her deeply as my hands slowly explored her smooth body. Softness and beautiful skin glowed under the light. She lifted herself up on her toes until our gazes were almost level, kissed me on the chest. Then dropped to her knees took my dick in her hand, stroking back and forth. My head fell back and I groaned at her touch. Her fingers traced along the edge of the tip, squeezing gently.

"Charlie," I grunted, watching her take control.

The task of concentrating on not losing my mind was getting harder and harder. With an alluring curl of her fingers, she wrapped her lips around my girth. Moving slowly, she clutched both of my thighs, her head bobbing up and down. I bent forward, pressing a finger in her ass, and listened to her moans.

"Ready for me, baby?"

Popping her head up, she nodded, still stroking my dick. I nudged her back on the bed and covered her heart shaped lips, clenching a hand around her neck while easing my hard length to her entrance.

Biting her lightly on the shoulder, I grunted at how tight she squeezed me. I shuddered in her arms, moving at an even pace. Charlie's sweet cries of pleasure soothed me, giving me an idea of what our future was going to look like now that Hector was no longer a problem. Seizing her lips, I brushed her hair away from her face.

"Damn, Nicco, my god!" I moved her up and down my rod.

"Jesus, Charlie, you're drenching my dick." I stood up, bouncing her around my dick. I smacked her ass gently and rubbed the sting away. I pressed a kiss to her lips and sucked her tongue.

"Shit! Fuck!" Charlie tossed her head back as I trailed my tongue down her neck. I pushed her up against the wall, kneading her ass.

Leaning in, I kissed her full breasts, and more and more I fell in love with her. "Baby, I'm about to explode. I can't hold it, Charlie."

"So, in love with you, Nicco. I'm coming too."

My chest tightened, my back stiffened, and I felt her come on my dick. We hadn't really talked about kids. At the same time nothing was done to prevent her getting pregnant.

Seeing her head fall onto my shoulder, I peppered kisses along her chin and jaw.

"We need to shower."

Her arms clasped around my neck. "Okay." She moaned as I slowly walked us into the bathroom with me still buried deep inside her, clenching both ass cheeks.

"Are you sore?" I asked, pulling her up from her hazy filled sleep.

"A little."

I pressed a kiss on her cheek. "We can shower and eat."

Charlie smiled. "You want me energized for another round. You're not slick."

I laughed, helping her to stand. "One more round after we eat, and then bed."

"Fine, tomorrow we have the party at your parents' house," she said.

My parents had the rented hall decorated with pictures of me growing up. My brother, as usual, was embarrassing me by showing off my baby pictures to anyone who would listen. Raising my hand, I slapped him on the back of the head when he picked up the one of me at prom with my date in the backseat of the limo. Feeling small hands around my elbow, I looked down and smiled.

"Are you having fun?"

I grinned. "I am." I stretched an arm on the lower part of her back.

"They mentioned you never liked big parties, but I wanted to show my appreciation on top of impressing your parents."

"Just be you." I cupped her lower back.

"Our moms are getting along well. Check them out." Charlie motioned to our parents laughing at my brother trying to steal from my dad's grill. When Charlie mentioned doing a simple dinner with my parents, I jumped at the chance to have them all together and we got closer as a family. The second I walked in the house and saw the silence, I knew something was up. Mom came in grinning wide, and I shook my head trying to turn and leave. Charlie caught me and begged me to stay and promised to give me another gift later tonight. All of my guys from work and their wives came out to celebrate with me. As soon as we locked up the Torrio case, more calls and messages came in from clients wanting to hire us. Aydin gladly promoted me to next in charge of the TN SEAL Security. If I wanted to branch off to open another location, I'd have his backing to run my own team. As for now, I liked being the third in charge, working alongside my best friends every day.

"You know the only birthday gift I want."

"I already know what you're going to say."

"What?"

"Me, naked. That gift will happen automatically tonight."

I smirked and tickled her left side. "No, silly. Waking up to you and knowing you're happy with me is the only gift I need."

"I am happy and grateful you are here with me." Charlie shoved her tongue down my throat.

"Get a room for you two!" my brother shouted, I flicked him off.

"He gets on my nerves," I grumbled.

Charlie laughed, slapping me on the chest gently. "Leave you brother alone and come eat."

"Charlie, thank you for the invite, and girl, the amount of single men around here. I am in heaven." Dedra fanned herself.

"Happy to help, Dedra." Charlie rolled her eyes.

"Oh, and happy birthday, Nicco." Dedra chuckled, waving us off, then switched to stand next to the guys from the office.

"Between Dedra and your brother, I have no clue

who is worse." Charlie picked up a plate for me and then her.

"Both are the center of attention."

Glancing at Dedra laughing dramatically at a joke my brother said, I had a thought. "Wouldn't it be funny if they got together?"

"Please save me from that torture."

"Come on, be nice."

"There's something I want to talk to you about." Placing the food down on the table, I scooped her hand in mine, walked off to the hallway, then pressed her up against the wall.

She extended her hands up my chest. "What's wrong?"

"I know you've had a hard time not doing your work."

"I'm okay."

"Still, I see when I leave you and you're home, you have that feeling of being lost."

Charlie bent her head onto my chest. "You are perfect."

"Nope, just attentive to my girl."

"Yes, you are."

"So tonight, not only are you celebrating me, I want to celebrate you."

She scrunched up her nose. "How?"

Reaching in my jacket pocket, I pulled out an envelope. "Here."

"What's this?"

"Open it."

Aydin and I talked again about me taking on my own team with more responsibilities. That turned into the discussion of opening more offices around the country.

"Nicco, you can't be serious." Charlie gasped, covering her mouth.

"I know it's not what you're used to designing, but at least you can keep busy until you figure out your next steps."

"You want me to design an office building for TN Security?" Charlie asked.

"Aydin is on board with me taking on jobs without him and Nasir. Having you beside me would feel great."

She jumped in my arms, and I squeezed her tight. "Is that a yes?"

Pulling back, she smiled, sliding her tongue in my mouth, cupping the back of my neck. "Yes, thank you for thinking of me."

"Your passion is designing. Anything I can do to help."

"Expected to give you a party and gifts, and I came out of your party with the best gift ever."

"Only gift I want is you beside me every day."

Charlie pressed a kiss on my lips. "Always."

The rest of the evening we danced, laughed, and hung around our family and friends. Leaving sometime in the early morning, we finished my birthday alone in bed exploring each other. Hearing her whimpers and moans, she gave me the best gift as she came on my tongue. Charlie's the light I wanted in my life and I plan on keeping her happy until my last breath.

Epilogue: Nicco

Three years later

Sitting in the SUV, I listened to the audio play of the subject we needed to grab before he tried to escape. Our latest case dealt with a gun dealer we've been searching for, for the past few months. At first, Charlie was hesitant about me taking the case, and I assured her I'd be fine. Listening to the recording, I signaled for the team to move in and I hopped out with Nasir and Knox beside me. Holstering my gun, we walked in a few seconds later to about five men lying on the ground with their hands up.

"We have enough to take him down for life," Jasper explained. I glanced around the front living room of the abandoned house.

Clapping him on the shoulder, I removed my earpiece. I felt my phone vibrate, so I stepped out on the porch.

Being with Charlie over the past three years enhanced my love for her to the point I couldn't imagine being away from her for more than a day or two. We often talked on the phone when I was out on stakeouts during the middle of the night, like right now.

"How much longer are you going to be?" Charlie questioned.

"Probably another thirty minutes, wrapping up now."

"You caught the guy?"

I smirked. "Don't I always?"

She giggled. "How much longer are you planning to be there?"

"You miss me."

"Always."

"Give me a few minutes and I should be home soon."

"Alright, but the food is getting cold and I had a surprise for you."

My brows knitted together. "What kind of surprise?"

She chuckled. "A surprise that needs to be told in person."

Lifting my wrist to check the time, I saw it was going on ten p.m. "You better not go to sleep."

She yawned. "Promise to wake me up?"

"Promise to wake you up with a big surprise."

We both laughed at the same time. "Nicco, you're nasty."

"Glad you know that, baby."

We hung up the phone after saying our goodbyes. Nasir handed over the paperwork as Knox directed the men into the back of the van. Police arrived a few minutes later and Aydin handled the questions. I hopped in the passenger seat next to Nasir.

"Drop me off first, man."

"Why? Usually you head to the office and debrief."

"I have a date."

"Charlie must have called."

Chuckling, I glanced at him.

"You two can't be away from each other for one minute without the other calling." Nasir shook his head.

"Aye, let's not talk about our girls. You know how high strung your girl is, bro." I laughed at the frown on Nasir's face. Starting the car, we drove off talking shit to each other until we arrived at my place. Jumping out, I waved goodnight and strolled up to the building, nodding at the security as I stepped into the elevator. A few minutes later I unlocked the door and lugged my bag to the side, amazed at the lights around the living room and music playing.

"Baby," I called out.

"Hi." Charlie stood at the entryway wearing a short red robe and holding a white envelope.

I removed my jacket and moved forward into the living room. I reached a hand around her waist, pulling us chest to chest.

"What's the surprise?"

"Since we have been together, you've struggled to take time out for yourself."

"Okay."

She handed over the envelope. "So, I planned a trip for the two of us." Prying it open I lifted two tickets to Paris.

"When did you have time to plan a trip?"

Charlie stretched her arms around my waist. "Amelia, Dedra, and I talked about doing a couples trip and thought it would be fun to get you out of the office for once."

I bent my head to peck her on the lips. "Paris with my love."

"You like the surprise."

Nodding, I caressed her lower back. "Anywhere with you is enough for me."

"Well, show me your gratitude, sir." She untied the belt on her robe and let it fall to the floor. She stood in front of me in only a thong and bra set.

"Being a fake boyfriend worked out in my favor." Cheesing wide, I picked her up in my arms, letting her legs wrap around my waist, and walked us back to the bedroom.

Months later in Paris

"Baby!" I walked into the hotel room, leaving my jacket, keys on the table. I pecked Charlie on the cheek.

"Hey, baby."

"Are you ready?"

"Yes, let me grab my shoes."

Our trip turned into a month-long trip of Charlie having the chance to make business connections. After Aydin locked her into designing a new office space, he recommended her to a few friends and she ended up getting an opportunity to grab some accounts in Paris and that made her want to start her own business.

"Did you get work done for the day?" I picked up a bottled water and took a sip.

Charlie popped up, pushing her sketch pad on the table. "I did, which means you have me all to yourself for the rest of the evening."

I winked and put the water down, pulling her into my arms. "Dinner."

"Dedra and Amelia told me to check out the museums while we were here."

"Once we shower and eat, we can do a little more sightseeing."

"I know work is getting busy for you. Are you okay with us still being here?"

I rubbed her back. "Aydin and I talked, and I'm not missing anything important."

"Thank you."

"Come on, we need to shower and get going."

"If we shower, you know we won't be leaving anytime soon," Charlie tittered.

I hunched my shoulders. "I like that plan, too."

* * *

I hope you enjoyed Charlie and Nicco's story. Check the Bonus scenes of some of my characters. Follow on the next page a sneak peek of **Knox**: A best friends sister romantic suspense, protective romance. Then hop into a sneak peek of a romantic comedy "**Something Earned**" book two standalone friends to lovers. More TN Seal Security series with a standalone, opposites attract, fake dating, military romance "**Nicco**"https://books2read.com/u/4DDn7k Are you a fan of sports romance? Then download one-night stand, billionaire romance "**Refuel**" https://books2read.com/u/b6Gaop Also, follow it up with workplace, sports romance "**Pressure**"https://books2read.com/u/bPeDqr

* * *

If you love romantic comedy, fake relationships, enemies to lovers, find it here, "**Something Gained.**" Click the link here https://books2read.com/u/baGLYy. My stories of friends finding love started with the Heart of Stone series that includes a host of characters and family. "**Broken**" book 1 Emery and Jackson a sports, one night stand, workplace romance is here: https://books2read.com/u/3LoelX

Then you can continue with a fun side story of Emery and Jackson with "**Valentine's Day**" short here: https://books2read.com/u/4jAypY

Jordan, her best friend's story, continues here in "**Rebirth**" book 2 a single dad, widow billionaire romance here: https://books2read.com/u/ba2OMx

* * *

Please also check out a second-chance workplace romance here, "**Renew Book 4**" https://books2read.com/u/4NXyPG with a host of characters intertwined.

Follow Desiree and Gabriel in "**Temptation**" a standalone contemporary, sports, curvy girl romance. Check it out here https://books2read.com/u/mle1Vv

Check out dark mafia romance here that started my journey with Antonio and Sabrina in "**Ruthless Book 1**" https://books2read.com/u/4AxKLo

The relationship continues in "**Savage**" book 2 as they get to know each other and their families: https://books2read.com/u/bpED6g

Antonio and Sabrina have more work to do in "**Beast**" book 3 right here: https://books2read.com/links/ubl/4AxKOd

* * *

Did you know **Janice and Carlo** have a book? Well grab this dark mafia romance with emotional scars, and betrayal right here: https://books2read.com/u/b6je6M

Any fans of forbidden romance, political? Check out **"Mutual Agreement"** https://books2read.com/u/mgzzWX a steamy romance. Do you love workplace romantic suspense? Then check out **"Aydin"** https://books2read.com/u/mBwaOy and the interconnected standalone hate to love, actress, damsel in distress bodyguard romance **"Nasir"** click the link here https://books2read.com/u/3Ln7Ee

Have you checked out **"She's All I Need"** click here https://books2read.com/u/49lkeW a sports, opposites attract romance. What about dark romance that has everything from steamy romance, opposites attract, suspense, thriller, celebrity, and more **"Stolen Book 1"** https://books2read.com/u/mvZlgV Don't miss the follow up Joaquin and Sofia's story in book 2 **"Saved"** https://books2read.com/u/4DWwLd

The conclusion for Joaquin and Sofia comes full circle in **"Betrayed"** here: https://books2read.com/u/4A5LGp

* * *

Catch up with favorite characters in this holiday short romance which includes spoilers. **"Holiday collection"** here https://books2read.com/u/bzd59G

For small town, single mom stories check out **"Until Seren**a" https://books2read.com/u/mej8vr. Always fun when you love billionaire romances so check in with

"**Cocky Catcher**" a sports romance, enemies to lovers here:https://books2read.com/u/3nGX55

Some familiar characters show up in "**Bossy Billionaire**" a workplace, enemies to lovers romance here:https://books2read.com/u/4E8JLg

All curvy girl, plus size romance lovers get into "**I Deserve His Love**" a standalone, second chance romance here: https://books2read.com/u/mVrGwP

The fantasy romance readers look no further than a "**Red Light District**" a curvy girl, fling romance here: https://books2read.com/u/m2RQ6G

Knox: TN Seal Security Book 4

She's his best friend sister, and now the senator's ex-wife – can things get more complicated?

It was a simple request from his best friend. All he had to do was pick Pamela up from the airport, but things quickly became much more complicated than that. For example, Knox's childhood crush on Pamela which he never acted on, is still there, only this time he can see she feels the same way.

If she were anyone else, Knox wouldn't have hesitated in the least, but with Pamela, there is too much at stake. And when he makes a move, he wants it to be right. Only keeping the senator's ex-wife safe is a little more dangerous than he expected because ex-lovers don't just vanish when you wave goodbye.

Can Knox and Pamela finally embrace their desire for each other, or is there too many factors keeping them apart?

This curvy girl romance will have you swooning over an alpha male that's afraid to commit, but can't resist his best-friend's sister. Go on, hit the one-click button now.

Something Earned: A Friends To Lovers

Kianna has worked hard and knows she deserves a promotion at the radio station, despite what all the naysayers in her life say.

Caleb has gone above and beyond to prove he can handle taking on more responsibilities at work. What he's not sure he's ready to handle is competing with Kianna for a job.

A promotion is up for grabs, but only one can have it. With ex-lovers, a relationship that's blurring the lines between coworkers, good friends, and lovers, Kianna and Caleb have a lot on their minds.

Can they ignore the outside distractions and focus on what matters, or will they jeopardize what could be the best thing that ever happened to them?

Heart of Stone Universe

Broken 1 Emery and Jackson
https://books2read.com/u/boWPAV
Heart of Stone Book 1.5
https://payhip.com/b/kWg7
Rebirth 2 Jordan and Damon
https://books2read.com/u/ba2OMx
Heart of Stone Book 3.5 Bottoms Up
https://payhip.com/b/HGP1
Reveal 3 Angela and Brent
https://books2read.com/u/31rx9l
Renew 4 Jessica and Joseph
https://books2read.com/u/4NXyPG

Struck Of Love Universe

The Early Years-A Prequel
https://books2read.com/u/49Zjnw
Ruthless Struck In Love Book 1
https://books2read.com/u/4AxKLo
Savage Struck In Love Book 2
https://books2read.com/u/bpED6g
Beast Struck In Love Book 3
https://books2read.com/u/3LpgdJ
Janice and Carlo Captivated By His Love
https://books2read.com/u/b6je6M
Brutal Struck In Love Book 4
https://books2read.com/u/4NQyE9
Stolen-Fuertes Mafia Cartel Book 1
https://books2read.com/u/mvZlgV
Saved-Fuertes Mafia Cartel Book 2
https://books2read.com/u/4DWwLd
Redemption Struck In Love Book 5
https://books2read.com/u/b5kZ8O
Betrayal- Fuertes Mafia Cartel Book 3
https://books2read.com/u/4A5LGp

Torn: The Carrington Cartel Book 1
https://books2read.com/u/mqXare?utm_source=
universal+link
Claim: The Carrington Cartel Book 2
https://books2read.com/u/bwyjPY

Also By Chiquita Dennie

Series

<u>Struck in Love</u>
The Early Years-A Prequel Short Story
Ruthless:Antonio and Sabrina Book 1
Savage: Antonio and Sabrina Book 2
Beastl: Antonio and Sabrina Book 3
Captivated By His Love:Janice and Carlo
Brutal: Antonio and Sabrina Booke 4
Redemption: Antonio and Sabrina Book 5

<u>Heart of Stone</u>
Broken, Book 1 (Emery & Jackson)
A Valentine's Day Short Book 1.5 Emery & Jackson
Rebirth, Book 2 (Jordan and Damon)
Reveal, Book 3 (Angela and Brent)
Bottoms Up Book 3.5 Jessica and Joseph Short
Renew, Book 4 (Jessica and Joseph)

<u>Cocky Billionaire Boys</u>

Cocky Catcher (Cocky Billionaire Boys Book 1)
Bossy Billionaire (Cocky Billionaire Boys Book 2)

The Fuertes Cartel

Stolen (The Fuertes Cartel Book 1)
Saved (The Fuertes Cartel Book 2)
Betrayed (The Fuertes Cartel Book 3)

Carrington Cartel

Torn: The Carrington Cartel Book 1
Claim: The Carrington Cartel Book 2

Something

Something Gained: A Romantic Comedy Book 1
Something Earned: A Romantic Comedy Book 2

Pierce Motors

Refuel:(Pierce Motors Book l)
Pressure:(Pierce Motors Book 2)

Summer Break

Summer Nights(Summer Break Book 1)

TN Seal Security

Aydin: Book 1
Nasir: Book 2
Nicco: Book 3

Standalones

Until Serena(HEA World Novel)
Temptation
She's All I Need

I Deserve His Love
Mutual Agreement
Scoring with Sadie
Exposed (A Bodyguard Novel)
Love Shorts:A Collection of Short Stories
Red Light District(A Fantasy Romance Short)

By Keke Renée:

Wet Heat
His Peace, Her Pleasure
Baby, It's Cold Outside
Love Don't Live Here Anymore, Book 1, 2
Every Time We Touch (A Wet Heat Novelette)
One Night Only- Love By Design Book 1
Cassian and Savannah Love By Design Book 2
Deidra's Love -Love By Design Book 3
Protecting Bria: Book 1
Protecting Chanel:Book 2
Protecting Yanira: Book 3
Haven: A Single Dad Romance
Sensual
Seek to Please: Book 1
Seek To Touch: Book 2
Seek To Bare:Book 3
Seek To Love: Book 4
Seek To Trust: Book 5
Seek To Earn: Book 6
Tease Me: Book 1
Promise Me: Book 1

By Ava S.King

Fatal Memory: Book 1 Teagan Stone
Fatal Target: Book 2 Teagan Stone

Fatal Crime: Book 3 Teagan Stone
Fatal Justice: Book 4 Teagan Stone
Fatal Enemy: Book 5 Teagan Stone
Fatal Death: Book 6 Teagan Stone
Fatal Revenge: Book 7 Teagan Stone
Fatal Pursuit: Book 8 Teagan Stone
Mirror of Lies: Book 1
Mirror of Lust: Book 2
Ruined: Andi Easton Book 1

Thank you so much for reading and if you enjoyed the crazy ride and decide to leave a review we'd truly appreciate the support..

About the Author

Chiquita Dennie is an author of Contemporary, Romantic Suspense, Erotic, and Women's Fiction.

Chiquita lives in Los Angeles, CA. Before she started writing contemporary romance, she worked in the entertainment industry on notable TV shows such as the Dr. Phil show, the Tyra Banks show, American Idol, and Deal or No Deal. But her favorite job is the one she's now doing: full-time writing romance.

A best-selling author and award-winning filmmaker, her first short film, "Invisible," was released in summer 2017 and screened in multiple festivals and won for Best Short Film. She also hosts a podcast that showcases the latest in beauty, business, and community called "Moscato and Tea." Her debut release of *Antonio and Sabrina Struck in Love* has opened a new avenue of writing that she loves. Nominated for 2021 Author of the Year, Best Black Romance "Mutual Agreement," and Best Interracial Romance for "She's All In Need". In 2022 nominated Author Queen of the Year, Best Black Romance "Nasir" Best Interracial Romance "Torn" and Best Romantic Comedy "Something Gained" by Black Girls Who Write.

If you want to know when the next book will come out, please visit my website at http://www.chiquitadennie.com, where you can sign up to receive an email for my next release.

What's Next?

Want to know what happens next?

Follow me on social media to catch the next release.

Reviews are the lifeblood of the publishing world. They're read, appreciated, and needed. Please consider taking the time to leave a few words on Goodreads, or bookbub.

Sign up for updates and sneak peaks at the site below.
https://www.bookbub.com/chiquitadennie
https://www.chiquitadennie.com
https://www.goodreads.com/author/chiquitadennie
https://Facebook.com/chiquitassteamyreadinggroup
x.com/authorchiquitad
https://www.instagram.com/authorchiquitadennie
https://www.Facebook.com/authorchiquitadennie
https://www.304publishing.tumblr.com

Acknowledgments

A huge thank you to my team that helps me behind the scenes, from my editors, test readers, graphic designers, and the list goes on. Truly appreciate each of you for keeping me on my toes.

304 Publishing Company

We showcase authors writing Romance, Women's Fiction, Thriller, and Erotic.Along with Mystery, Suspense, Poetry, Beauty, and Style Books. Thank you for taking the time out to visit. Join our mailing list to stay updated with new releases and blog posts.